Run Me To Earth

PAUL YOON

SCRIBNER

LONDON NEW YORK SYDNEY TORONTO NEW DELHI

First published in the United States by Simon & Schuster Inc., 2020
First published in Great Britain by Scribner, an imprint of
Simon & Schuster UK Ltd, 2020
This paperback edition published 2021

Portions of this text were previously published in slightly
different form in *Harper's Magazine*.

1 3 5 7 9 10 8 6 4 2

Simon & Schuster UK Ltd
1st Floor
222 Gray's Inn Road
London WC1X 8HB

www.simonandschuster.co.uk
www.simonandschuster.com.au
www.simonandschuster.co.in

Simon & Schuster Australia, Sydney
Simon & Schuster India, New Delhi

A CIP catalogue record for this book is available from the British Library

Paperback ISBN: 978-1-4711-9058-2
eBook ISBN: 978-1-4711-9057-5
eAudio ISBN: 978-1-4711-9147-3

Printed in the UK by CPI Group (UK) Ltd, Croydon, CR0 4YY

For Ethan Rutherford,
for Laura,
for Van (1931-2019)

Author's Note

In the 1960s, during the war in Vietnam, Laos was engaged in its own conflict between the Communist Pathet Lao and the Royal Lao Government. In an attempt to suppress the spread of communism across Southeast Asia, the United States—using the Central Intelligence Agency—provided extensive support to the RLG.

The CIA's paramilitary operation included training ethnic groups—in particular the Hmong—to fight alongside the government and then, later, carrying out aerial bombing missions over the country. These bombing missions would last nine years (from 1964 to 1973) and would end up totaling more than five hundred and eighty thousand. This is the equivalent of one bombardment every eight minutes, twenty-four hours a day, for nine years.

Over two million tons of ordnance were dropped on Laos—more than was dropped on both Germany and Japan during the Second World War. Thirty percent of these cluster bombs, or "bombies," failed to explode on impact.

While *Run Me to Earth* focuses on this time period and these events, its story—and the characters and the situations depicted—is an act of imagination.

PY

I have worn the fur of a wolf and the shepherd's dogs have run me to earth...

—W. S. MERWIN

ALISAK

(1969)

At the farmhouse, the three friends asked each other where they went to at nights.

They had finished most of their duties for the day and were sitting down on the floor together in the corner of the long room that had, two decades ago, held dances and lavish parties but had now been converted into a ward.

"A ship," Prany said. "I go to a very large ship."

"Someplace where there is a working fireplace," Prany's younger sister, Noi, said, leaning back against the wall. "A very large fireplace." Noi had been disappointed to learn that all the fireplaces in this house had been found sealed up when the doctors first arrived.

Above them there was a gap in the ceiling where they could see two stars and the passing clouds. In front of them, at the end of the rows of cots, a woman tried to turn in her sleep, forgetting that her legs and her torso had been eaten alive when she stepped on an unexploded cluster bomb three days ago. Then the woman remembered what happened but she avoided looking down, watching instead the moonlight coming in through the tall windows that lined the far wall.

They kept the curtains open because those who couldn't sleep wanted to look outside at what was left of the distant valley. It was called the Plain of Jars because of the strange stones scattered across this part of the country as though a mountain had fallen from the sky and shattered.

As far back as they could recall, Alisak, Prany, and Noi had heard so many stories of the megalithic stone jars they weren't sure which one was true: whether they were intended to collect rainwater for travelers, whether they were used to make wine for warriors who would return from great battles. It was also said that the jars once belonged to giants who roamed these hills. And others thought the jars had nothing to do with this earth at all and that in some future time someone or something would come back for them.

When the first bombs dropped, Alisak, who had been working on a farm that morning, was so stunned by the sound he was unable to move even as the horizon dispersed into a wall of smoke. His first thought: *They've come for the jars.*

These days he laughed at that. That old life. From the gap in the ceiling came the faraway engines of airplanes, and he waited for the detonations of the cluster bombs somewhere west or north of them. There had been so many bombings— it was getting more frequent, he lost count of how many a day—he almost didn't notice the sound anymore.

4

A birdcall, which he never heard anymore, would be stranger.

The sky flashed and flashed. Eventually, Alisak knew, maybe next week or in a month, the bombers would come back around toward the house. Not for them, but again for the roads and the valleys.

Yesterday, Prany packed bags for them, hidden now under a loose floorboard in a bedroom upstairs. He managed to stash one of the house pistols, too.

"Alisak," Prany said, leaning across, clutching a pillow, and poking him. "You didn't answer."

Alisak forgot they were playing the game. He was worrying a blister on his palm from the handlebars of the motorcycle he had been riding all day. The blister had burst and the flap of skin had turned almost as pale as the moonlight catching their boots.

"The desert," Alisak said. "I go to the desert."

Noi tipped her head back. She thought this was hilarious. She stayed that way, laughing quietly, her mouth open like a fledgling bird that was about to catch something from above.

"In the next life," she said, "our friend will be a Bedouin."

"What's a Bedouin?" Prany said.

Noi hit her brother on the head and then the two curled themselves around the frayed, embroidered pillows they had found upstairs on a bench beside an out-of-tune piano. A sheet of Bach was still on the piano's stand, the pages yellowed, but the bars and the notes were clear and dark.

The siblings tried to sleep, their limbs making scratching noises on the marble floor as they settled. If it rained they would have to move, but through the course of the year they had become better at predicting the weather, and tonight they bet it wouldn't. The gap was perhaps the circumference of a jar in the valley. They liked looking up at it. If the sky was small enough, there was less of a chance of an airplane crossing over it. If the sky was small enough, it was just the sky.

Alisak stayed up, watching Noi, then watching the beds, first shift. If something happened, if someone tried to rip the IV from their arms and leave, or if someone screamed because the morphine was exiting out of their bodies, he would have to run down the hall past the six mirrors on each wall that caught his movements until he found a doctor or a nurse.

Most of them were in the kitchen, sleeping in whatever privacy they could imagine as they lay on a counter or on the floor, in a closet or against the angle of cupboards, having drunk enough whiskey to knock themselves out. Some of the staff had even begun to take the morphine themselves, the ends of a suturing thread from an operation still wrapped around their fingertips like a good-luck charm. And sometimes, resting on their open palm, as though they were perpetually ready for surgery, there would be a scalpel.

For this, for keeping watch and for keeping the ward clean, for assisting these people who were trying to save as many civilians as possible in a war that had been going on in various forms for almost all their lives (and for riding the motorcycles), they were paid more American dollars in a day than they could earn in six months on the streets of Phonsavan.

They had even learned some English and French this year from the Vientiane doctor they called Vang. He was perhaps in his thirties, if that, wore glasses he kept misplacing, and, as it turned out, was not only proficient in several languages but played the piano.

In the ward, when his two friends were asleep, Alisak practiced saying some French phrases to himself as the sky flashed with another detonation and the woman on the bed placed an arm across her eyes, her mouth slowly moving as though she were practicing the language with him.

He wondered, as he often did, about the Frenchman who once lived here. He—the Frenchman—was a captain from the Second World War, had retired here and gotten rich off the tobacco fields around the property that no longer existed. For Alisak, he was all rumor: a drunk and a womanizer who

7

spent his days in a long silk bathrobe waiting for his next party to begin; a man who had stayed in this country for much longer than most of the French and whose allegiances could be bought; who, early in the war, let North Vietnamese soldiers use his fields as a route on their way to the southern parts of Vietnam.

How much of this was true? Alisak, entering a room, would sometimes pause, wondering what his days and routes were like within this house that was the size of a small village.

Noi had in fact met him once, Alisak only at a glance, long before they knew who he was. He pulled up to them on the side of the road one day and had asked if he could hire Noi to help in the kitchen at one of his parties. So she had gone with him, though she refused to speak much about that evening. She only shared with Alisak the bits of conversations she had overheard from the partygoers—*Did you ever notice the river is changing temperature?*—and that the man was very strange. That, and her regret at not eating more of the food she had been hired to carry on silver trays.

Noi had been twelve. In the rare times she mentioned him at all, she called him the Tobacco Captain. So Alisak had begun to think of him that way. Strike a match. Captain of not much, just ash. This man who had lived alone in this house he had built for himself with all its windows that revealed all the distances. A house that even now, as a skeleton, seemed to Alisak as grand and mysterious as a temple.

In her sleep, Noi slid across, thinking Alisak's lap was a pillow. She was dreaming; he could sense the shudder of it as if she were leaping. She twisted up slightly, and he stared at the rise of her hip, that angular bone, began to reach for it but changed his mind, suddenly self-conscious of the fact that he hadn't bathed in a week. He looked away. Her hand fluttered. And then he reached down and turned the old ring around her thumb that she had found somewhere and never took off because she often did this herself, when she was troubled or when her mind was far.

And as her body calmed and she rolled back to her pillow, he also wondered, as he often did, if anything had happened to her at the party. And if something did, what that was. He tried to remember the car and that man inside, calling them over. And that he himself had stood there doing nothing, staring at the man's money and then, a moment later, staring at her leaving in the car.

Twelve.

If that man were here, Alisak would kill him. These days he could. For that matter, Noi could, too. They could use a syringe full of air or a scalpel to find a quick vein. They could lead this Tobacco Captain across one of his own fields that were now covered in unexploded bombs, stand back, and watch to see which of his limbs blew out first as though lightning had struck a tree.

They had been told of or had seen things like that. They had grown stronger, running about through the ruin of this house, lifting heavy boxes and empty shell casings. And, to their surprise, they had also become healthier, with food that wasn't much but was much more than what they were used to.

They drove the motorbikes. Noi was a better rider than him but always let him lead, pretending she wasn't. Some sense of courtesy or humor alive even in all this.

There was a painting upstairs that Alisak thought looked like her. A girl by a river. A basket of fish hanging from the crook of her arm. He had never seen Noi with a basket of fish and probably never would, but it looked like her: the dark hair, the posture that held a sense of both shyness and confidence. He had considered taking it down and hiding it, to keep it for himself.

Supposedly, the paintings that remained on the walls were famous and stolen. Alisak caught an aid worker one night taking one out of its frame and rolling it up. His eyes never left Alisak. Then he walked past, whistling, and tapped Alisak's head with the canvas like he was a drum.

What painting had that aid worker taken? He tried to recall this, seeing a hill in his mind.

They were around the same age, Alisak, Prany, and Noi, and they had once lived next door to each other on a different hill, in a small settlement on the outskirts of the town, where the space between their houses was the width of a motorbike's handlebars. Where they were aware of the sound of each other behind the perpetually damp walls—the sound of their bodies, the clatter of their makeshift kitchens in the corner, their voices calling to play, calling for help—aware of each other's shadows outside their wooden doors long before they had a sense of a greater world beyond that slope, that river.

Then they had cared for each other when there was no one else to care for them. Alisak's parents eventually succumbed to the opium they were lured to farm; the siblings, who had no memory of their mother, lost their father early on in the war, when he was hired by the government to fix a bombed road two days' journey south but was caught by the Pathet Lao. He was told to walk the road as the soldiers took bets on whether he would step on a bomb, grew bored when nothing happened, and shot him. Neither Prany nor Noi was certain of anything for weeks—their father was often gone—until the peddler who passed through every season came to the hill, asking for them.

It was when the fighting intensified, after that encounter with the Tobacco Captain, that they began to wander the country, always staying together, sleeping where they could, finding work where they could, avoiding the armies where they could. They spent three years surviving the rainy seasons, the sudden approach of strangers, and a war where the boundaries shifted endlessly, where they often jolted awake from the sound of bombers or the sudden appearance of an army in a town or a village they were staying in.

When a jeep appeared that day to recruit them for the hospital, they had only recently returned to their own town. They hadn't meant to. It was just that there didn't seem to be anywhere else they could go anymore.

Alisak and Prany were now seventeen, Noi a year younger. It was the early fall of 1969. Their last season together here. Or at least that was what Vang told them. That they would in all likelihood be evacuating soon.

Alisak never said this out loud, but he felt as though he could stay here with them in the madness of this house forever. He thought there would be nothing better. Paintings, mirrors, pillows, and tall windows. A kitchen and a piano upstairs. The three of them always together. The great motorbikes.

Their answers to the question of where they went to in the evenings, in their dreams or when they were awake, as they tried to keep their minds off the denotation flashes coming closer and getting louder, and the steady flood of the maimed and the wounded, were always different.

Where did they go at nights?

A museum or Paris. The moon. A cave, an endless beach. They had been doing this since they were children.

No one ever said home.

Some days, Alisak thought he would miss the bikes more than he would any of the people they worked for at this field hospital. By his count there were about twelve personnel he could recognize and whom he had grown accustomed to helping. Some of them were Thai, others were Hmong and from the mountains, and many of them were from the lowlands, south. All of them were allies of the Royal Lao Government and spoke some mix of Lao, Thai, Hmong, English, and French, always adding hand gestures.

Save for Vang, however, Alisak's interactions with everyone had been brief and in the orbit of chaos. A nurse shouting at him, *Hurry up, boy, hurry and bring the tray over. Dammit, don't spill, that's the last we have of it. Shove the bit between his teeth and hold it down, harder, believe me, he won't feel his teeth breaking.*

So Alisak did, standing behind the injured boy whom he thought he recognized from the town, and talking to him. He pointed up with his chin toward that corner of the roof that had fallen from the concussion of a bomb one month ago in order to give the boy something for his pale eyes to focus on instead of his own body.

It was the rainy season. The rain came in furious bursts, never lasting for more than a minute, but it felt as though the roof wouldn't be able to hold the force of weather. They watched the miniature waterfall in the ward that lasted long enough for Vang to amputate a leg above the knee. They would use the pooling rainwater to mop the floors.

Sometimes, as the rain kept falling, Vang walked over to that corner, slipped off his gloves postsurgery, and washed his forearms and his hands. Then, like the flip of a coin, the sun returned. As though it never rained at all, catching the rim of Van's eyeglasses. And Alisak, not realizing he was still holding the ends of the wooden bit, woke from where he was, felt a nurse unlocking his fingers as she told him he could go.

The truth was that this Lao doctor, Vang, seemed different from the others. He was the only one, Alisak thought, who had the ability, when he addressed them, to pull them out of the world that was consuming them. If that were possible in the panic that never seemed to end, in the voices and the detonations across the valley that always caused another bit of the house to collapse.

Once, a wounded farmer tried to flee, having no memory of the cause of his injuries, shouting at everyone that he had entered some kind of war prison and had been tortured. He had run down that hall of mirrors straight past the kitchen and grabbed Noi by the hair, assuring her that he would help her, that it was all right, that he was here now as he tried to drag her out of the house.

He took her as far as the entrance hall. Then, for unknown reasons, he let her go and ran across the tobacco fields entering the valley. They waited for a buried bombie to go off but nothing happened. They never saw him again.

The ceaseless sound of the house, the people, the bombs. Alisak had learned to almost think of it all as the rain. Or that was what Vang had once told him, snapping his fingers and ordering him, in French, to repeat the phrases as though he were no longer in this country but somewhere foreign and far.

(They had all gotten better at conjugating verbs—*Coudre! Couds! Coud! Cousons!*—and listing Parisian landmarks as Vang took them along on a quick tour around the city in his mind. How did he know Paris? They would never find out.)

Other days, he played the piano for them. It was upstairs, in the corner room where they—the three lost orphans, as Vang called them affectionately, referring to an ancient children's story everyone knew—took turns as lookout, panning across the valley for movement with a pair of binoculars and a rifle as their ears were invaded suddenly by the foreignness of a few bars of Bach.

Wild, reckless notes that Alisak felt under his ribs. Spaces of quiet.

When Vang wasn't there, Alisak would flip through the stack of music sheets that had been left behind, trying to decipher the coded symbols for himself.

Vang was never able to finish what he was playing. He adjusted his glasses that almost always slid down his nose as he ran out to answer another doctor shouting for him. Or, he rushed into the room where they had brought in a radio so that they could communicate with the government or with the Hmong fighters who, if they could, relayed back the advancing positions of the Pathet Lao and the North Vietnamese.

Mostly, though, Alisak, Prany, and Noi kept to themselves, performing the tasks they were assigned. Or they were away, riding the motorcycles, following each other and the route they made into Phonsavan, where there was another hospital that had been set up.

There was also the river where they could pick up supplies that were delivered by an old woman operating a boat. They had known this boat woman since they were children, and their parents had known the woman because they used to buy food from her. It had also been a way for them to travel. They rarely ever spoke to her—Prany was convinced she was actually a mute—but when they were younger, she used to let them ride with her upriver past the villages. If they helped her sell, she gave them extra food or some money and brought them to the riverbank, where they jumped off the boat without her ever stopping.

She was still alive, still with her boat, and still silent, though she didn't have any extra food now. There was instead a rifle in a basket by her legs, Alisak not knowing if she had ever had the reason to use it.

They carried pistols when they were on their missions but they rarely had the chance to fire them. Here, the fighting on the ground had for the most part ceased after the majority of the roads had been bombed, and because of the rain, so they had in the recent months encountered very little of the armies. Instead, there was the new landscape the fighting had left behind: abandoned tanks in the fields, trucks split in half in a muddy crater, clothing, unidentifiable bones that were bright as steel, weapons, cases of ammunition they quickly loaded onto their bikes, and empty shell casings they could bring back to collect rainwater.

Now, in this corner of the country, everything happened from the air, from the side that was supposedly theirs. There had been times when they were forced to outrun jets flying low, the pilots unsure of who they were, whether they were enemies, the three of them with their faces wrapped in bandannas like bandits as they sped quickly into the woods and vanished under its thick canopy.

They stayed a full night once in the woods, sitting on the ground by their bikes and listening not to the rain, which fell silently, but to the endless torrent of bombers somewhere above the canopy that seemed so close they kept expecting one to crash down on them, cutting off the tops of the trees. They had never seen an airplane up close before and a part of Alisak wished one would come down. He wanted to see where the bombs were stored, how they were released, what a pilot did to release them. What kind of person a pilot was.

In the woods that night, they didn't sleep. They huddled under the thickest canopy and tried to ignore the rain seeping through their clothes. They reached out to soak some stale bread they had found in the kitchen, to soften it, and passed it around, biting off pieces. *Couds, cousons.*

At first light, they returned to the town that had for the most part remained intact, though hardly anyone was there anymore. Yet they continued to raid and scavenge, in case they overlooked places: in the cupboards and closets of the café where there was a half-torn propaganda poster depicting a monk standing beside a soldier, both of them with their fists raised; in the rooms of homes or the guesthouse they would never have dared entered years ago, where an old, blind woman hid behind a door and listened to them walking around. Or in the restaurant behind which they used to loiter with the stray cats, waiting for a cook to give them some leftovers. Alisak remembered how Prany always fed the animals, their teeth sometimes breaking his skin, though Prany never seemed to mind, wiping the blood away with a silk handkerchief he had untied from the collar of a dead dog when they were wandering the south.

What happened to that handkerchief?

In the town the next morning, after scavenging for supplies, they hurried to the other hospital, where a terrified doctor, who appeared as though he had crawled out of a cave from another century, handed them one last box of morphine. He had wrapped it in his doctor's coat because the box was soaked from the rain and about to fall apart.

"Tell Vang there's no more," the doctor said. "Please stop coming. Leave us alone. We can't help anymore. We can't help."

He hurried back inside. He had spoken to them like the beggars they had been. Noi took out her pistol and aimed it at him, at the glass door that was still there, beyond which they watched the man returning down a corridor with some kind of limp. When he was gone, she fired, shattering the glass. A nurse who had appeared in the lobby screamed and ducked behind a man she had been pushing in a wheelchair.

Noi would have fired again if Prany didn't remind her they needed to save the bullets.

Noi kicked the hospital door once for good measure. Prany claimed the doctor's coat.

When they drove back to the farmhouse, all the windows dark because the electricity had gone out again, the nurses, even Vang, tried to hide their surprise as they lifted candle flames toward them in the hall, thinking the three of them had run away, or that they had died.

•

The bikes were BSAs. British. Birmingham Small Arms Company Limited. Alisak often said that out loud to himself, wondering where in England Birmingham was. They were three decades old and ran perfectly. Alisak was unsure how the bikes had managed to come here, but like the piano and the art, and just about everything in the house, they had already been here, in a garage, when Vang first arrived to take the place over.

The bikes were lighter than they appeared and had enough stability to handle the terrain of the fields and the hills all the while being fast and maneuverable.

There was a fourth courier, as the nurses called them— never the orphans—but he missed the line of sticks they had planted to indicate a safe route by half a meter and triggered a bombie. He—the fourth—was from the mountains in northern Thailand near the border and he had come across the Mekong to help, having cousins in the area.

They used to speak together in that mix of languages. He knew good jokes. Was a good singer and knew some card games they didn't know. He wore on his right wrist a woven bracelet he said his Auntie gave him. They thought he was referring to his relative, an actual aunt, until they realized, hearing the woman's voice on the radio one afternoon, that it was a nickname and that she was someone Vang communicated with. When they pressed the young man further about who this Auntie was, he wouldn't say anything more.

That was all they knew about him. He was older than them and Alisak thought Noi was a little in love with him. He would watch the way she avoided looking at him, which was something she never did; she wasn't shy.

That day on their bikes, Prany and Alisak were too far ahead to realize what had happened, but Noi heard the loud pop, like the air around them had broken, and then there was nothing, only the pieces of the bike, the front wheel, released from its body, still spinning forward.

They stopped, all of them, and did what they had been told to do. They walked carefully into the smoke that was misted in red—that color they had grown so accustomed to it didn't startle them anymore—and salvaged what they could: parts of the bike, clothes they could find that were still wearable, the backpack. Then they stored it all in one of the stone jars in the field so that they could pick the things up on their way back.

(A decade later, in another country a world away, Alisak would enter a festival on the bay of a hill town and, as music blared and people danced, he would watch a man hold up a can that sprayed red, would watch him graffiti a seawall, and he would hold his breath, not realizing, for a moment, what exactly was coming out of the can.)

They learned from the dead. They adjusted where to place the sticks in the ground, the three of them fanning out barefoot across the valley to better feel the ground. Around the back, where there used to be a garden at the end of a slope, they created a circle so that the helicopters from the Royal Lao Government could land safely and take away as many of the wounded as possible.

•

It was seven months ago when the American bombers that had been aiming for the roads missed their targets, striking locations close to the farmhouse. It was like the entire valley had erupted and was breaking apart over them.

We're on the same side, you idiots!

Only Alisak heard Vang screaming this as he grabbed the doctor's waist and tried to prevent him from opening the second-floor window and leaning out into the roar of wind and the debris hurling toward them. The sky suddenly gone, replaced by smoke and fire. The bombs dropped across the Plain of Jars, reaching the north wing of the house, the entire roof and the wall collapsing there, burying five people.

It took a day for Alisak's hearing to return, for his legs to calm so that he could stand and look for Prany and Noi, whom he eventually found hiding together in a bedroom closet, their bodies folded over each other and their eyes shut even as Alisak leaned down to touch them.

Everyone in the house was trapped. Their only access in and out of this area to find food and supplies—to find any survivors who were wounded—became the bomb-ridden field, which the three of them began to explore, slowly, every day, using the bikes and walking. They came back—every day they made it back—to find a stack of money on top of the piano for them.

Ten days ago, as Vang predicted, they learned through the radio that the American planes were coming again and that the hospital would need to be evacuated. There was the promise that the government would send helicopters. So far, four had arrived but they didn't know how many more would come. Or what would become of the wounded who were unable to be moved. Only that the hospital workers had agreed to stay for as long as they were able to.

Vang began to make the ones who were too injured to transport as comfortable as possible. He kept the curtains open if a farmer wanted to look out or shut them if a townsperson wanted to sleep. He gave a woman from a hill village as much morphine as she wanted—he gave all of them, if they were able to eat, his ration of food. If they wanted it, they were bathed more often, Alisak bringing in the rainwater they had been collecting outside in the shell casings they had propped up near the side.

No one had yet to tell the three of them where they were going. They were assured it was soon and that Vang had acquired them safe passage out.

But where?

Prany thought it would be either Chiang Mai in Thailand or farther, to somewhere in France.

Prany wanted to go to France. So did his sister. It would make sense, they said to Alisak, because Vang had been teaching them French. They wanted what he had described to them: French cigarettes and wine and bread and the Seine. The museums. All those gardens and monuments.

Noi thought they should steal a painting and bring it with them before they were all gone. She said everyone was now doing it. She said she saw a nurse do it yesterday, take one down from the wall, cut the canvas out of the frame, and roll it up.

Alisak said what if the men in France were all like the Tobacco Captain, but Noi wasn't convinced of it. They couldn't recall if the man eventually returned to France during the war or went somewhere else. Or nowhere at all. He could have drunk himself to death in one of these rooms. The husband of a Phonsavan woman might have come and murdered him and buried his body.

"The woman herself might have," Noi said.

The Tobacco Captain was gone when the Vientiane doctors took the house over two years earlier. Some of the staff, however, came back, helping the doctors, helping run the house that was falling apart, that no longer had water or a garden, only intermittent electricity. They helped for as long as they could, until they gave up, left, or died.

When Alisak, Prany, and Noi were recruited months later, they were asleep in the shade of a tree beside the river. Alisak heard the jeep first. It was an RLG jeep, and two nurses walked up to them with an envelope full of money. The nurses spoke to them in Lao and then Hmong, not sure which they would understand. They understood the Lao better.

"Can you drive motorbikes?" the nurses said.

It was afternoon, and for a moment the sky was quiet. They had only been back to the town for a few days, and they were starving, dehydrated, their bodies numb. They had been waiting for the boat woman to appear in the hopes she had some food. Alisak was in the thread of some dream. Some mountain road he kept walking down, passing animals and seeing a coast in the distance but never getting there. By then, they had been living and surviving with only each other for so long that it took them a moment to understand these strange women in their uniforms were unthreatening.

Only Prany stepped toward them. He examined the money. U.S. dollars. He licked his thumb and flipped through the bills because he had seen a man do that once at a gambling house. Then he tightened the headband he had made for himself from a torn shirt and said, "Miss, for this, we can fly."

He was pleased by his humor. It made Noi laugh.

But not the nurses. They opened the door of the jeep. Across the river, a house that had caught fire in the morning had finally crumbled into a mound. It belonged to the family of a monk. A thief had burned it down in anger after hearing a rumor there was treasure hidden inside but found nothing. The monk had come down to the temple that was still open, and before heading to the farmhouse, the five of them watched from inside the jeep as he lifted the hem of his robe, revealing his sandals, and walked around the smoldering debris that had been his childhood home.

France or Thailand. Alisak felt indifferent about the not knowing and the where. Everywhere seemed far and foreign. It had been more than a year now since they had moved into this farmhouse, and he couldn't recall the last time he had been in one place for so long. Where there was no one telling him to go.

He had grown used to the house. The wounded. The chaos that was so plentiful it was less like rain, he thought, more like a silence.

He was good at driving. Knew the bike now, he thought, better than he knew himself. Knew how it turned or sped or hesitated and groaned. He could pick up a farmer who had lost his legs faster than anyone, slip him behind, hold on to his arms as they raced back to the hospital before the man bled out. He could do things like that. He knew how to find veins and he knew his suturing threads.

What would he do somewhere else? What did he do before? He laughed at this, too. He was a cook for one week at a café. He bicycled a rickshaw. Sometimes, he sketched the faces of farmers in the fields in a notebook and asked if anyone wanted to buy them. Near Vientiane one year, when there was a period of calm during a rainy season, he stood outside a gambling house and didn't let in anyone the owner didn't want inside. It never worked, he was a child, he was all bones and short—he still was—so he was beaten.

He was beaten so often for smelling rotten or for begging for food or because of the way he was dressed or simply because it was easy to beat a child. All this in wartime. He fought back, got cut four times, swallowed his own tooth once, and waited a day thinking it would exit out of him—that he would get it back—and then wept when he searched for it in his own shit, alone, in a field, and it wasn't there.

His own tooth had vanished somewhere inside of him. There were times this fact bothered him more than his own hunger or the sudden volley of gunfire.

What did Prany and Noi do before that was better?

They all lived lives where they kept losing things. Sometimes even each other, for days, because someone had hired only one of them, or they were caught in the opposite ends of a field, hiding, their voices useless in the deafening, unbearable air, the three of them afraid to look or to stand above the level of the high grass.

He wished he could take a BSA with him. He pictured them remaining in the back of the hospital beside the dead tobacco plants. He imagined them surviving everything and the years, ruined by the weather, sunk into the ground, but there. He imagined coming back for his. Listening to the breath of its engine. The handlebars where bits of his blistered palms were probably stuck like dust. The gunpowder smell all over its body. He could never stop the shaking in his knees until he got on his bike.

Wherever they ended up, he would get a new bike. Noi and Prany would get one, too. They would all race the way they did across the valley even though they weren't supposed to. But they did, coming back, knowing the routes now, the farmhouse rising up out of the horizon. An enormous stone jar that maybe a giant made standing there untouched, carrying rain from the night before. Probably an undetonated bombie floating in there, too. Or a flash of color in the water that they knew was human.

Another helicopter roared in and down, the wind so strong as to feel impossible, and Vang, behind a second-floor window, during his first break in three days, delirious and unable to sleep, to keep his body quiet, rushed a melody on the out-of-tune piano.

•

Alisak was upstairs, scanning the field with a pair of binoculars when a figure emerged from behind a piece of large stone. He thought perhaps it was someone coming to them for help.

This happened every day. People attempted to walk across

the valley to reach the hospital until Alisak or the others had to rush out with a bike and get them, all the while shouting at them not to take another step forward. Which someone always did.

The man in the distance, however, wasn't a stranger. He wasn't military either, which they were always fearful of, that one day they would head out on their bikes and it would be a trick. That the Pathet Lao or the North Vietnamese would be there. That they had always been there.

But the man now crawling around the field was, in fact, Vang. For a moment, Alisak thought he was wounded. Or deranged. The doctor had finally become deranged.

He held his breath as Vang crossed over the line of sticks and entered territory they knew nothing about. It was a minefield. Through the binoculars, he watched as Vang settled himself down against another large, broken piece of stone. Behind him, on a short ridge, stood the remnants of a tank they had, last season, managed to safely reach and rummage through, taking the pistol that was now in the room next door, under the floor with their backpacks. The tank's long, slim cannon pointed out across the distance like the arm of a tree.

The doctor waved, a slow arc, and it was then Alisak realized Vang was drunk, the empty whiskey bottle beside a nearby tree stump in the field.

Alisak felt someone's breath on his shoulder and turned to see Noi looking out past him. She rested her chin on his shoulder and took the binoculars.

"Shit," she said.

He felt the weight of her there against him. He inhaled. She had just washed her face. She smelled like the awful, powdered hospital soap of which they only had a bag left and had been sharing among the three of them, pouring water over each other's heads as slowly as possible. This morning he woke in a mess of limbs, uncertain of who the arm over him belonged to, the leg, whether it was Prany or Noi as his fingers grazed an ear. He kept his hand there, touching the softness of the lobe—in all this around them, every day, the earlobe was always soft—not yet wanting to get up, wanting this moment to go on.

They slept like young animals in a den, he realized, and had been doing so for as long as he could now remember. He didn't know how to tell someone how improbable it seemed to ever want to sleep alone again. The vacancy of it. He had nothing, had always had nothing, but he had them. Today, he had the bike. He still had Vang.

Noi gave him back the binoculars and he returned to watching the doctor, who was now searching for his glasses in his shirt pocket—they were not there—and then squinting down at the ground beside him, his hands sweeping across the dirt.

In recent days, when the helicopters started to come with more frequency, evacuating the wounded, some of the doctors had brought up the last crates of whiskey and wine the Tobacco Captain had left in the basement. They had gone through most of it quickly and, in their exhaustion and their hunger, quickly vomited most of it out.

Vang must have saved a bottle and wandered out at night, unaware that he was doing so. Or fully aware. As unlikely as that was to Alisak, it was possible. Over the past year he had watched so many stumble out like the delirious farmer who thought he was a prisoner, so many ignoring the pleas as they entered the far fields, wanting only to go back home, not believing there wasn't one anymore.

It seemed a miracle the doctor was still alive.

Prany came in, holding a bag. They were splitting the cash they had been earning and saving, and he folded it in whatever extra clothes he had found today from the dead. In the other bags under the floorboard were six packs of cigarettes, six tins of some kind of fish, two for each of them, and knives or a can opener, and matches.

A round of detonations began. They couldn't see the planes but the distance blinked like there was a lightning storm in the morning light. Briefly, the tank was illuminated like some large animal against the sky.

Prany flipped the coin he always carried. Heads or tails. Alisak won. He flipped it again. Prany won and again Noi said, "Shit," and tucked her pistol in the back of her pants. Then she tied a bandanna over her head, the glow of her washed face gone, and spun the ring around her thumb once.

Prany took the rifle they kept in the closet and pushed open the window slightly. He checked to see that the weapon was loaded and clean and adjusted the scope.

Alisak kept the binoculars and looked out again at Vang, who was still waving and now singing a song Alisak couldn't remember the name of, only that there was a record of it in the kitchen.

"He's a better piano player than a singer, yeah?" Prany said.

Ignoring him, Alisak scanned the front of the house, waiting for Noi to appear. They stopped using the grand main entrance with its columns. They simply stepped out where there had been a wall seven months ago, over the mound of rubble and the broken cots, and where they now kept their bikes.

He heard the engine starting up. Noi drove out slowly, taking what had been the main driveway and turning right into the field that had once grown tobacco. Beyond that lay the Plain of Jars, and where Vang was now trying to sit up, curious, hearing the motorcycle engine. He kept singing, in English:

Moon river wider than a mile
I'm crossing you in style someday . . .

If Prany were a better shot he would have told him to fire a warning to make Vang sit back down. He almost took the rifle himself, but he didn't want to risk it either. He kept track of Vang wavering, the way the doctor gave up and sat back down. He scanned back to Noi on her BSA, beginning to speed in between a row of dead plants, entering the field.

But he couldn't find the sticks they had stuck into the ground to guide them. Alisak's breath caught in his chest and the panic began to set in. He tried to concentrate on his breathing the way he was taught to do. The binoculars had become slippery from his sweat and he gripped them harder. Then he noticed Noi was riding parallel to a line, which meant she had found them, her knee almost touching the sticks. The ends of her bandanna flapped slightly.

He thought this would calm him but it didn't. He kept squeezing the binoculars. In his periphery, he spotted Prany scanning the distance with the rifle, across the broken pieces of jars around Vang, some as tall as the homes they had been born in.

Noi reached him. Or reached a spot as close as it was possible. The doctor was suddenly delighted by her presence and stood, singing more loudly, lifting his arms and bellowing as though he were in an opera.

Stop!

Noi, yelling, lifted her arms in front of her, palms out. Alisak would never know if it was her or her voice or something else, but the doctor's expression changed just then. He froze and, in a moment of sobriety, Vang seemed to understand where he was and the situation he had put himself in. Now, through the binoculars, Alisak caught the tremors beginning in the doctor's limbs. First his knees and then his wrists.

(Loose wrists, Vang once said, playing the piano, Alisak not sure what he meant until now.)

Vang covered his face with his hands. His mouth was open but no sound came from him anymore. He tried to keep still. A line of drool spilled down from his bottom lip.

"I don't want to look," Vang said to Noi.

He didn't mean it about himself. He was talking about Noi. She had taken off her shoes. She left the boundary of the sticks and stepped forward into the unknown field, where Alisak could already see some bombies that hadn't dropped hard enough to go off or to sink underground, their smooth surfaces reflecting the daylight like points in water.

Alisak and Prany watched all this from the second-floor window, through their respective lenses. They watched Noi move across upturned earth and broken bits of stone, the soles of her feet searching for patches that appeared untouched. She would be avoiding the feel of a hard, curved surface under the dirt as much as she could. Every time she stepped forward, she dug her heel in, leaving a solid footprint she could follow back.

Alisak wanted to scream.

She was two steps away when another round of denotations started in the distance, perhaps a little closer, concussing the air. Alisak felt it, Prany did, too. It was like a ghost had passed through his chest. He looked through the binoculars as Noi stepped closer, and then the doctor, shouting, stepped forward and ran to her.

Alisak shut his eyes, held his breath. Waited. No pop. Nothing. When he opened his eyes, he saw the doctor embracing Noi and crying, and then they were walking back with Vang behind, his arms wrapped around her waist as she led, retracing her own steps.

Prany kept the rifle pointed out as his sister helped Vang onto the back of the motorcycle and returned across the fields, the bike running over a pile of dead tobacco leaves and rounding the side of the house.

Still no airplanes approaching or men on the ground.

Prany, his face inscrutable, returned the rifle to the wall and hurried down. Almost at once, Alisak heard a scuffle downstairs, someone shouting, and knew Prany had struck Vang, or attempted to, and then there was silence for a little while.

Alisak stayed in the piano room, holding the binoculars. He waited for Noi to come back up, but she didn't. Then he fell to his knees and vomited the little he had eaten an hour before. A pale, bubbly puddle that was already vanishing through a crack in the floor.

He wiped his mouth with his wrist and hurried down to the room next door. It was covered in wallpaper that was peeling and had an empty metal bed frame. He crouched near the frame and lifted a floorboard. Below were three backpacks and a pistol wrapped in a cloth.

"I can't be here anymore," he said, not realizing he was saying this out loud. He was breathing heavily. He took the gun and slipped it behind his waistband.

He couldn't be here, he said again. Everyone would be all right. Noi and Prany would be all right. They would have each other. The doctor would be all right.

Slinging a backpack over his shoulder, he stood, grew nauseous again, rested for a moment against the bed frame. He focused on the painting above the headboard. It was the one of the girl by a river, the hem of her skirt drawn up above the water. He could cut the painting out of the frame right now, he thought. He could roll it up and sell it and live off that money forever. He could do that, and he wasn't sure why he didn't. He had never even touched any of the paintings, as though someone had told him he never could, and for some reason he had listened.

He imagined Noi, older, holding a basket of fish in France. Maybe Prany would be the one painting her there by a river. Someone else. Not him.

He stepped over the empty bed frame and stood very close to the painting, close enough to see the brushstrokes and the old pigments. His hands were shaking. They had been shaking since he had entered this room. He thought it was his knees, because it was always his knees, but it was his hands this time, for the first time. He didn't know what to do.

Maybe it wasn't France but Thailand. There were times this year when all he did was imagine their futures, but stopped himself before he went too deeply in. Now he did. Or he attempted to. He kept pushing his mind forward, from a day to a month to a year, but the more he tried the more he couldn't. He saw nothing. In that moment, he could imagine nothing.

He reached up and touched the painting. Pressed his fingertips against it. Felt the ridges of the brushstrokes. Then he returned the backpack and the pistol to the space under the floorboard.

Outside, it was like the sunlight was blinking. Daylight lightning. From downstairs, from the bottom of the steps, he heard a voice shouting, "Helicopter."

A moment later, the same voice said, "I found them," referring to Vang's glasses.

•

One night during a rain shower, before they knew for certain that they were leaving, Alisak noticed Noi sitting beside the woman with the ruined legs. They were talking. There was only the light from the windows, so their shapes were vague in the dark. Every so often he could see the arc of Prany's flashlight panning over the rows as he checked on each patient and then walked over to the hole in the roof, where water was coming down. He saw Prany open his mouth, the flashlight catching his chin briefly and the falling water striking his lips, bouncing away.

They had been instructed to change the woman's bandages as often as they could, to keep the festering wounds as clean as possible. He had stepped out to retrieve what turned out to be the last pack of bandages—no one knew if any more were coming, possibly from the next helicopter—and he had paused at the threshold of the ward, watching for the first time the woman talking to one of them.

Now, as he approached, Noi and the woman left whatever world they had been in together. He gripped his flashlight with his teeth and shone it down on her body. If this sudden light bothered her she didn't show it. She was in that moment of clarity during the morphine before she usually slept, and he didn't know how much longer she would be awake.

"I remember you," she said as he unbuttoned her shirt, Noi helping him, both of them careful not to touch her skin. Not because it would hurt her, but because their hands were cold and they were aware of the heat of her and didn't want her to feel the shock of temperature. Alisak began to peel away the bandages across her stomach, lighting his movements with the flashlight in his mouth. Prany was still standing in the corner, his back to them, looking up.

"I remember the two of you," she said.

It turned out she was a basket weaver who shared a stall at the night market once a week in the town with a potter from her village. The potter's goods were heavier. If the potter couldn't borrow a truck he carted his wares himself on a wheelbarrow down the hills. If they went together, she helped him.

"That night I didn't," she said. "He had gone down ahead of me. He wanted to shop for a gift for his daughter. It was her birthday the next day. We did that. We sometimes got something from the town because our children always wanted something from the town. My baskets. They're light. They're sturdy, but they're light. I slip the handles over a pole, twenty of them, and I carry the pole across my shoulders. Easy enough. I follow the road. I love the walk at the start of night. I love the low stars and the fields and the smell. The smell. What is that smell? I haven't smelled it since. Lovely air. Deep grass. It's my only time alone. My husband is taking care of our daughter. I am alone. The road passes some homes on a slope. Before you get to town. Shanties. Metal roofs and some thatch ones and narrow doors following the slope and a maze of paths. You of course know. I saw you both there. You were sitting on the branch of a tree together near those homes, looking out across the slope. You didn't notice me. I passed under you and I saw you lean over and whisper something into his ear. Yes, you. To him. Tell me: What did you say to him?"

Alisak had removed the entire bandage and had begun dabbing the wounds with ointment. He and Noi looked across at each other. He had no memory of this. He wanted the woman to keep talking as he cleaned her stomach.

42

"We have this game," Noi said. "We imagine someplace we would like to go. We were talking about that."

"I sold seven baskets that night," the woman said. "The most I ever sold. It was a great success. Have you seen my baskets? They are light and sturdy. I can give you a discount."

"Yes," Noi said. "We would like that."

The rain came down harder. And then came the wind. Prany, his feet soaked, turned as though someone had called for him. He walked over, leaving his wet footprints across the length of the floor, and stood nearby, watching as Alisak changed more of the woman's bandages and then moved down to her thighs and her shins. Prany was restless with his flashlight. He kept panning it across the room.

"I walked back the same way that night but you weren't there," the woman said. "Up in the tree. Carrying thirteen baskets. You see, I thought you were spirits. You brought me luck. That is why I remember you. That was what I believed. That you were spirits who brought me luck."

"Boo," Noi said.

The woman smiled. She reached for Noi's hand.

"Yes. Boo. And luck."

"What was the gift?" Noi said.

"The gift?"

"The potter. His daughter. The birthday gift."

"I think it was a bracelet. From the market. Red and yellow. He traded it for a teacup he had made."

She didn't let go of Noi's hand. In the distance, the air began to concuss. Dust fell from the corner of the ceiling, widening the gap a little more.

"Where do you go at night?" Prany said.

He was helping Alisak now, talking to the woman. Alisak's mouth had gone numb from holding the flashlight. Prany gripped his own with his teeth to replace Alisak's and together they stood at the foot of the bed, cleaning her.

"Khit," the woman said.

They didn't know where that was. They had never heard of a place called Khit. Now they heard airplanes.

"The smell," the woman said. "I can't smell it anymore. It was so lovely. The night. Deep grass. Walking alone. Only thirteen baskets. You can carry thirteen forever. I want to walk."

The woman slowly shut her eyes. Alisak, who had been avoiding looking at her face, finished dressing her legs as the rain stopped.

•

Wake up.

The face of the doctor filled his vision. In his half sleep, he thought it was Prany and Noi's father. Perhaps Alisak had been dreaming of him, he could no longer remember. Perhaps he had been thinking of the man who had taught them how to drive a motorbike.

Vang was wearing his glasses and sober. It was three days after, but Alisak wasn't sure what hour it was until he found a window. He was lying in the corner of the main ward, hugging a pillow, his back against the wall. The gap above him. He was alone and it was the start of evening. He caught a star through the windowpane and then the sound of more bombs, louder this time, rattling the metal tray on the stand beside him.

Seven of the beds were still occupied. He watched the nurse who recruited them pumping the seven with morphine and then trying to hide her crying as she hurried out of the room.

They were going. Alisak understood that suddenly. He looked around for Prany and Noi. Then he got up and walked over to the woman who had spoken to them. He stared at her, convinced he would, years from now, remember her. She stared back at him, in the haze of the drug.

"Don't forget the wheelbarrow," she said, and smiled.

He wouldn't remember her face, but he would remember he didn't have the courage to touch her in that moment—not even her elbow or her shoulder as she kept smiling as though watching a band at a café. Maybe in the morphine she was.

The house rattled again, and he felt Vang take his wrist.

"Teach me another word in French," Alisak said.

"No time," Vang said, and pulled him away. "Come on."

He wanted to know where his friends were. Vang assured him they were just up ahead as they hurried down the mirrored corridor. In the mirror, Alisak saw he was still carrying the pillow as though he were a child. He dropped it, fixed his hair, and tucked his shirt into his pants as he followed Vang.

He didn't even know whose clothes he was wearing. He had long ago gone through the ones he had arrived here with. Against the wall were three gurneys occupied by more who would be left behind. Following Vang, he passed through the kitchen, where the other doctors were emptying cupboards in silence, packing what they could in duffels, tucking kitchen knives into their pockets.

Alisak caught Prany in a far corridor. He told Vang he needed to head upstairs, but the doctor gripped his arm, and they kept going. He felt the house shake. Voices filled the air. Then it was the blades of helicopters, one already leaving as they entered the destroyed wing where they kept their bikes, the wind suddenly gripping his shoulders and pushing him back.

He leaned forward against it. His bag was next to his bike. Prany's bag next to his bike, Noi's next to hers. Noi and Prany themselves were outside in the dark, helping some people into the aircraft.

What time was it? He wasn't sure. It could have been evening or not yet morning.

"It's the last one," Vang said, shouting into Alisak's ear over the sound of the engine. "No space left. We'll head to another exfil point. They'll pick us up there. I'll ride with you."

The helicopter took off. The wind blew dust and old leaves and debris into the room. In the corner, behind pieces of the wall, were bits of the outside that been collecting there for months. It looked like a nest.

Noi and Prany came back, got on their bikes. Noi had tucked the pistol in her waistband. One of the nurses got on Noi's bike, carrying Noi's backpack. One of the doctors who had been rummaging through the kitchen joined Prany. Alisak handed Vang his bag.

"France or Thailand?" Prany shouted.

"What?"

Vang couldn't hear. He didn't answer. They started their bikes. Alisak's stalled. Alisak motioned for Prany to go ahead and he tried again. The sky flashed as his engine came to life. He drove out and Noi followed, all of them turning on their headlights and entering the tobacco field. The wind blew over them again, not from the helicopter now. A burst of rain.

Alisak turned to see the windows of the main ward one last time, searching for the woman, but there was only the rain spraying on the glass. The sun was rising invisibly behind the clouds. They were drenched. In between the denotations was the sound of the far helicopter. And then there wasn't. They increased their speed, Prany in the lead, Noi behind Alisak.

So they were leaving. They were suddenly gone. He looked briefly back over the doctor's shoulder at Noi. He thought Prany must be pleased to be out front. Prany kept speeding up, eager perhaps, and Alisak blinked his headlight for him to slow down in the rain. But Prany didn't, he sped across the valley and soon he was a good distance away from the two of them.

He wanted to turn to see where Noi was, but with Vang behind him he knew he shouldn't. He followed the sticks and soon they were passing where Vang had woken up three mornings before. Or was it four mornings before? He had lost track of the days. Days and time. His eyes were sore and bloated. He felt the sting of one of his blisters opening again, unable to heal.

In the far distance, more bombs detonated. They could see the bombers now. They were flying parallel with the bikes but still far, gliding over a mountain range as though they were ancient birds. It was almost beautiful. It embarrassed Alisak that he thought that.

The rain thinned. Good. He tapped the handlebar with a finger, ignoring the pain of the open blister. He increased his speed, hoping to catch up with Prany, but mindful of the mud that was now everywhere. He drove over a bump, but he remembered it, had driven over it before. The bombers were no longer visible and the sky began to clear, bringing color everywhere. He passed an empty farm and a few stone jars that had survived, intact, as tall as houses, and others that were demolished and pulverized. Two women stepped out of a small open shed as though they had been living there and shouted something indecipherable, waving a pale shirt.

He made out a tree line in the distance. The wind. He waited for the rain to return but it didn't come. He had lost Prany over a slope and then he found him again, far away, a small, dim path of headlight in the valley.

France or Thailand. A river and fish.

He felt a tapping on his chest. He tried to ignore it, focusing on their safe line of sticks, but then looked down quickly. Vang's fingers were tapping Alisak's body manically. Alisak didn't understand what was happening. He tried to ignore the tapping. And then he knew. Vang was humming and pretending to play the piano.

It suddenly occurred to Alisak that the doctor had not been on a motorbike for this long before. Or had never ventured this far out from the hospital since he had arrived. Alisak shouted at him to stop, but Vang didn't respond. He tried again. The tapping was distracting him. He grabbed Vang's wrist and tried to pry the hand away down to his waist, but Vang clawed hard against Alisak's chest. He kept his hand there in a way that scared Alisak. Or a feeling close to it. He tried again one more time, pulling down hard on the doctor's hand, not realizing the bike was tipping to the side from the shifting weight until he sensed a slipping and turned to see Vang, wide-eyed, mouth stunned open, sliding back, clawing for him. Finally, he spotted Noi's headlight, closer than he thought she was. Close enough to briefly see her startled face as she swerved, breaking away from the safe line of sticks to avoid the doctor, who was falling now, and then the blast happened—bright, close lightning, there was that pesky ghost in his chest again—and as Alisak was propelled into the air, there was only the dirt and the start of morning.

He was unaware he couldn't hear when he got back up. He thought he was hearing everything. Thought he was standing when he was lying on the ground. Then he stood, wiped the mud from his eyes, and checked himself. His head, his chest, down to his legs. No wounds. No breaks. No blood. Through the dense smoke, he walked around in a small circle, searching. He rubbed his eyes. Then he thought he spotted a headlight racing ahead.

It made him hurry. He coughed, stumbled. Bright spots cascaded across his vision and then vanished. He walked a little farther in the smoke and found his bike. It was okay, the bike. The engine still running, a wheel spinning. It was a good sign. A lucky sign. He looked across to where he thought he had seen that headlight. He thought it must have been Noi racing ahead, and laughed. The laugh felt good. No, it felt great. He shouted and clapped. He punched his chest and laughed loudly. He wiped some more mud off his face and kept looking around. Vang. Where was Vang? There. Not far at all. He grabbed Vang's wrist and helped him back onto the bike. He asked if the doctor was okay.

No time. He raced across the field, not waiting for a response. He felt Vang's hand against him and was relieved the doctor was no longer pretending to play the piano. He sped up, ignoring his dizziness, the bright spots that came back. He found that headlight again, in a far field. It appeared now to be heading in the opposite direction, back toward the farmhouse, but he quickly lost it. He wondered if it was something else. An animal? *No time.* The land was brightening even more. The air. His eyes not yet used to it all. Squinting, he followed the last of the safe line until he made it to the road toward the town and went faster.

In the schoolyard, not far from the river where they used to sleep by the tree, two helicopters, Hueys, were idling. He thought the bike up ahead was Noi's, but it wasn't. It wasn't a bike at all but a jeep. Alisak dismounted and entered the wind of the blades. He could hear everything. People were running by him and getting in. The first Huey took off. A man rushed over and led Alisak to the second one.

Alisak shouted, asking where Prany was. Where Noi was. Every time he opened his mouth it was as though he were swallowing the wind. He couldn't hear himself. Then he realized, only now, that he couldn't hear the helicopters either. He heard only a ringing, a loud bell.

Where are the others?

The man stopped. He reached across and unclasped Alisak's fingers. He picked up the hand that Alisak had been holding and threw it across the schoolyard. He lifted Alisak up into the Huey and buckled him in. The helicopter was full. He tried to recognize someone but they were all shapes pressed up together in the dark. He kept looking down at the hand on the concrete. Severed below the wrist, it was mud-covered, its fingers slightly curved as though it had been holding something.

And then, around the thumb, a silver glint. Or perhaps he was mistaken, he wasn't sure anymore. He wanted to shut his eyes, to shout and jump off, but he did nothing. He couldn't move. He heard only the bell. Then that, too, was gone.

The silence was wonderful. It was like an embrace, the softest blanket around him. He tucked himself into it. The ground beneath him shifted like water. The sky kept flashing. He wondered if the sun was plummeting, breaking apart. He thought that would be fine. Because the wind was all over him, and that was like a blanket, too. He had never been so high up in the air before.

For this, I can fly, he thought, but forgot who said that.

As they took off, they lingered over the yard and then turned to follow the shape of the bright, trembling river, past an old boat tied up to a post, past the remnants of the monk's house, where a dog stepped over a fallen door and, for a time, galloped after them.

In an anonymous air base, he was hurried onto a large cargo plane and traveled for a lifetime.

Alisak slept and woke and changed airplanes at other air bases, seeing the outside for a minute—some flat sliver of unreachable landscape beyond a fence, a million stars thrown onto what looked like a heavy dark sea above him, always the wind—and then he slept again, unaware that he was crossing India and then Saudi Arabia.

The hold shook, but it was also him shaking, uncontrollably, his hands, his limbs. He sensed someone touching his wrist and he jerked his arm back. Then he felt the handkerchief the man beside him had offered mysteriously, as though Alisak had been crying or because there was something on his face to wipe away.

Is there something on my face?

He didn't open his eyes. He didn't open his eyes for hours. Afraid to look at anyone, afraid of what they might look like, what condition they were in, what they were missing. He said it was just like a tree getting struck by lightning, but no one responded.

In his blindness, he folded the handkerchief into a thick band and tied it over his eyes, the length just long enough to make a small knot behind his head. (There, better.) He turned to the person beside him and then the one on his other side and asked what part of them they were missing. He said it was okay, he knew how to stitch them back together.

He unbuckled his belt, got up, and, still blindfolded, navigated the narrow aisle like a drunk, then suddenly like a dancer, growing more confident in his blind steps, creating something close to a flourish with his arms. He clapped and shouted. The more the plane shook, the more he was able to move freely. It was as though he were in space, afloat.

He taunted the other passengers, shouting that he had all of them, both his hands and both his legs, all his fingers and toes.

He was whole!

He asked if the plane was carrying a wheelbarrow. Then he skimmed past a wall of wooden crates, attempted to climb them until a pair of arms wrapped around him tightly and dragged him back to his seat as he screamed and struggled and kicked.

The snap of a buckle.

"You are a stupid boy," someone said close to his ear. "A stupid boy."

They let him keep the blindfold on.

Hours later, after they had landed again, he thought he was changing airplanes when a man led him onto the tarmac and took him across, holding him the way a father would. He recognized the smell of him as the man who had given him the handkerchief.

The man began to whisper commands in French. "Walk straight, keep walking, there, careful, watch your head," and then Alisak was settled into the back of a car.

He let the man untie the handkerchief for the first time in days. Sunlight shocked him. It was impossibly bright and blue everywhere. Above him, a large-winged bird followed the wind over the rooftop of a building. In the air was the smell of something deep and old. He pushed through his own haze and tried to focus on the back of the plane to see if anyone else was stepping out.

Where were the others?

"What others?" the man said. "Remember what I told you. Be good. Work well. Live. Do what you were good at. You're here now."

He had no memory of anything the man had told him before this. He didn't even know who this person was. He shifted his focus onto the features of this stranger, but then the car started, startling him. He reached for him, but the man shut the door and stepped back, not going with him, so that all Alisak would ever know of this person was that he kept him company from one airplane to the next, that he had a pale handkerchief that once smelled of perfume, which he let Alisak keep, and that he was now receding, standing on the tarmac and waving.

There was a tremendous ache in Alisak's eyes. He was dehydrated, sleep-deprived, disoriented, and nauseous from the sudden speed and the turns of the car. The driver, an older woman, glanced at him through the rearview and spoke to him in Thai. Her skin was dark and thick from the sun. It was like the desert. She was wearing sunglasses that kept slipping down her nose.

"Where are we?" he said.

He couldn't fully understand her, so he had switched to French.

"Perpignan," she said.

He had never heard of Perpignan.

"France," she said. "Southern France."

"Not Thailand?" Alisak said.

She laughed. In the rearview her mouth hung open, revealing the front teeth she was missing, another capped in gold. She introduced herself as Karawek, though she went by Kara here. She was Thai, had been here already for years, helping people like him.

"People like me," he said, though he was unsure if he said it out loud.

He had never seen the ocean. They were suddenly driving beside it. It was everywhere and flat and sky-colored. He got lost in it, out there, beyond. Some layer of him inside began to leave him, through his fingertips, his eyes, his mouth. Leaning against the window, Alisak began to cry. Not because of the water. Karawek pretended not to hear and turned on the radio, driving slower, passing by a headland where there was a church. Stone houses and then a seawall where a boy was sitting on the ledge, fishing. Far away, a red boat was moving slowly, following the coast. Then the car turned away and they were driving inland toward the mountains.

Karawek said he could open the window if he wanted. He rolled it down, was met by the wind. It dried his face. He was getting used to the brightness. The heat felt different here, it was thinner, more dry. They were driving by an orchard. And then, without warning, an abandoned cottage, the roof collapsed. Beyond, in a pasture, goats watched them.

"How do you know him?" Karawek said.

He had been clutching the handkerchief, but now he folded it, following the visible creases, and slipped it into his pocket.

"Who?"

58

"The Seabird. Yves. The Vineyard."

"The Seabird?"

She didn't go on. They arrived at what he assumed was the Vineyard, the woman driving up to a large barn at the base of the mountain. He saw no vines. On a nearby slope, on the ridge, was a large stone house. Karawek handed him a card with a Marseille address and told him if he ever needed her, to call.

He thought she was leaving, but she took him in using a side entrance. They were in the shade of a corridor, and as Alisak turned into a room with square bales of hay, the tallest man he had ever seen stood from a desk where he had been writing in a notebook and, ducking under the hanging lamp, approached.

"Ah," the man said. "So you are the one who has been wreaking havoc on my brother's motorcycle collection."

Before Alisak realized what was happening, he was embraced, his entire body swallowed by the largeness of the third stranger he had spoken to today. The man's medical coat cocooned him. It masked the daylight. He breathed, smelling something wonderful. Cleanliness. He couldn't remember the last time he had bathed. Standing there on the threshold of the room, he grew self-conscious of his body, his stink, and of his weakness. Some vague memory of a blind walk down the cargo hold of an airplane slipped into him and vanished.

He yearned for a plastic bag of the powdered soap he and Prany and Noi had washed with. The way, wet, it would create a layer of mud on their faces so pale that roaming the halls of the farmhouse, they had looked like monsters in the mirrors, frightening the nurses, and each other.

He pressed himself into the stranger as though wanting to vanish. The man didn't resist.

"I told you," Karawek said, still in the corridor, finishing her cigarette, her voice an echo. "The Seabird."

She extended her arms to mimic the span of the man's. Someone else, someone new—a young woman, a glimpse of pale hair—appeared in the corridor and greeted Karawek. They were all looking at Alisak.

Motorcycle collection, he thought. He realized only then, in the silence afterward, that he was in the arms of the Tobacco Captain's brother.

•

Alisak lay awake in the night. The narrow window overlooked the fields where there was once the vineyard. A sliver of the barn. He was in a second-floor room of the stone house on the ridge. Living a year in the chaos of the farmhouse, he knew when he was the only one awake. Or believed he did.

He would never get used to this new silence. The new

noises. The creaking and the broken parts of a house that he was told, hours ago, was now a clinic for the people who lived in the mountains. His role would be similar to what he did at the farmhouse. He would walk down to the converted barn every morning and help. He would sleep upstairs in the main house.

He left the room, headed down, found himself in a kitchen. On a counter there was a cloth covering a plate with bread and some food that looked familiar to him—like wet grapes—but that he couldn't identify. He slipped one into his mouth, trying to recall what it was, having no memory of its taste. The salt of it shocked him, the pleasure of the oily layers, of biting into the meat before his teeth hit the seed. It was delicious. He ate another, suddenly ravenous. Unsure what to do with the seeds, he pocketed them, tucking them into a fold in the handkerchief.

It had been days since he had eaten. He tore off a heel of bread and poured the water that was in a clay jug into a mug and drank. Scanning the moonlit room, drinking more water, he oriented himself: a wall with a framed map of somewhere, the faucet dripping and making a hollow noise as the water hit the sink. A frayed towel folded carefully on the counter and a bowl of lemons. Old books someone had shoved into a gap in the wall where there were once stones. He leaned toward the leather spines bloated by the weather, reading the French, not knowing all the words. Through a narrow gap in a window frame, the air came in. The night.

In the room beside the kitchen, by the end of a long table, there was a piano. It was identical to the one at the farmhouse. For a moment, he believed it was the same one, that somehow it came with him on the plane, and so, holding the piece of bread in one hand, he knelt and popped open a wooden panel under the keyboard and stabbed his arm into the upright's insides, his fingers searching the dark space for the mementos they used to hide in there.

Then, still eating, Alisak headed outside, not noticing in his hunger and his new surroundings that the door was already ajar. The night was clear. He was met by a low, enormous moon the color of fire. It brightened the entire length of the land in a paleness, and he stood in front of the house aware of his surroundings in a way he hadn't felt since he had arrived.

He was aware of the pair of shoes sticking out into the moonlight on the bench across from him, the rest of the person in the deep shadow of a tree. He had smelled the cigarette earlier and now in his periphery he could make out the pinpoint glow of the bud in the dark like a slow heartbeat.

He sensed no threat in that corner. He understood the person wanted to be alone. So he focused on the fields as the sound of a faint engine cut the air, recognizing it as belonging to a motorcycle. He gripped his hands together. Then with an open palm he hit the side of his head.

"Good," he said. "Okay."

He made a soft noise and hit the side of his head again. He continued talking in French, practicing some phrases out loud. Then, in English, he sang, briefly, *Moon river wider than a mile* . . . The shadow on the bench kept still.

From somewhere far he pulled the knowledge that it was his birthday soon. It was his birthday, but he couldn't remember in this moment what day exactly. Whether it mattered. As he felt the moon on him, the cool of the elevation, his birthday made him think of his father. It surprised him, that he thought of his father at all.

Alisak searched for the thread in his mind that created that bridge. Before his father began working in the opium fields, he had been, for a time, a land surveyor. For Alisak's birthday one year, his father made him a map of an imaginary town on an imaginary mountain. There were endless streets and alleyways. A maze of buildings and doors that led nowhere and everywhere, up into the sky and down.

Some need for that, suddenly. Something plucked from a child's dream.

He hummed: *I'm crossing you in style someday* . . .

The left shoe under the bench shifted.

Yves, he thought. *Yves, the Seabird. Karawek. Vang. Prany. Noi.* He repeated the names. He walked across the ridge toward the tree. He approached the bench and picked up the shoe on the grass and slipped it on the person's foot. Sitting on the bench was the young woman who had come in to talk to Karawek earlier in the day. He recalled nothing about her other than she worked here, too, and that she was older than he was, already in her twenties.

She had not moved. She offered him her cigarette.

"Mostly they come in for broken bones," she said, in French. "They fall off their horse or their tractor. You wrap up their torsos and tell them there isn't really anything we can do with ribs. If it's something we can set, then we'll set it. If it's something we aren't equipped to handle, we'll call the hospital in the city."

"What do you call this here?" Alisak, who was speaking back to her in French, took out a seed from his pocket.

"*C'est une olive*. An olive seed."

"And what is your name?"

"Marta."

"Marta," he said. "Olives." He poked the side of his head and counted with his fingers: "Yves, Karawek, Vang, Prany, Noi, and Marta."

"What?"

"And Khit. I think that was a name. Yes. A name. The weaver. The basket weaver. She said a name. I wonder if she's still there. Lying there. We left her, you know. We left her there. I should have given her some food. Rice. Bread. We had bread there. Someone could make bread."

"You're tired."

"Yes."

"Go back to sleep. There's nothing to do tonight."

Her voice was slippery to him. It was as though she were slowly moving away from the bench even though she wasn't.

"The olives," he said. "They're so good. Where are they from? I want to eat them every day."

"You can. It's okay here. You'll be okay here. We promise. You'll be safe."

"Safe."

"Yes."

"This is France."

"Yes."

He suddenly remembered the game they used to play. About where they went to at nights. He looked up at the sky, trying to remember his answers.

"Where are the others?" he said.

"Asleep."

"I really must find them."

"The patients? They're asleep. They're down there in the barn. Only a few farmworkers in the area tonight."

Marta stubbed out the cigarette and looked up at him from the bench.

"I don't think so," Alisak said. "Not the ones I'm looking for."

"Who are you looking for?"

He leaned forward so that their faces were almost touching. He hadn't yet bathed and he could tell she was trying to ignore the smell of him. He could smell her soft cigarette breath, could feel it brush against him, could almost hear her heart as he cradled her face and squeezed a little, tilting her chin up toward him.

"Did you know?" Alisak said. "I am a Bedouin."

Marta remained silent. Her bottom lip trembled. She stayed where she was, without turning, as Alisak walked around her, down into a field, leaving the house and the property.

He entered the woods and began, in the late night, to climb the mountain.

AUNTIE

(1974)

In the mountains, when she was hungry, she sewed.

There was often a basket of clothes nearby wherever she was staying, and so the woman who was called Auntie would pick out a pair of trousers or a shirt and spend an hour mending some tears in the fabric or sewing on buttons.

It was easy to find clothes. You took it off the bodies. Or you found them hanging from what was left of the trees. Or they were on the face of a boulder, spread out and weather-faded, as though someone had been in the middle of a wash only to vanish. Other times, they were in perfect condition, wrapped up in waxed cloth in the corner of a hut, perpetually ready for a journey. Clothes of all sizes. Clothes a decade old or a few days old.

With the good shirts, Auntie cut off the bottom button and saved those, because it was harder to find buttons. And yet, over the years, she had managed to collect an assortment—dull wood, pale bone—and these she carried with her at all times in a pouch on her waist.

She had no appetite this morning but Auntie crossed the space of the hut and selected a shirt, unfurling it in the air, the snap of it breaking the silence. Early daylight leaked through the wall slats, catching the cloud of dust that hung heavy around her. The shirt, a boy's shirt, was torn in places and stained—even a wash couldn't get some of the splashes of color out—but it was wearable.

So as Auntie waited for news to come up the mountain, as she knew any moment now it would, she sat on the floor and laid the shirt across her lap. From a pouch, she took out a handful of buttons and spread them out beside her, looking for a few that might match.

She leaned forward a little and then leaned back. She could see the dirt under the raised floor of the hut better than she could see the buttons. She wished she had a pair of reading glasses. She wished it because four years ago she had tried a pair on for the first time in the camp where she had been in hiding with Vang and Prany before it had been raided and burned. That distant fire was visible for days as she trekked across and away from that high mountain as quickly as possible, not knowing who had managed to escape, whom she would see again, or how.

She could no longer remember whose reading glasses they were or why she had tried them on. Only the clarity and the sudden joy of it, even then.

That was the last time she had seen Vang and Prany.

It felt like she had been collecting buttons forever. In the hut, she selected one that had the shine of bone and began to thread it into a space where a button had been. It was badly matched, but it fit the hole and would hold. She worked slowly, being careful with the needle that she kept hidden in the cuff of her own shirt because it could work just as well as a weapon.

Movement came from outside, then a shadow passed under the hut, navigating the stilts below. Too small to be a child. An animal, perhaps. Then, footsteps. The splash of a cup in the plastic buckets of rainwater they had been collecting.

Auntie kept sewing. She pricked her fingertip, wiped the blood on her trousers—a pair she had found one day on the body of a man who had starved himself hiding in a cave, his body embracing a boulder, as though desiring only that embrace—and finished the button and started another, picking up a darker one, coconut, perhaps. She hadn't eaten since yesterday afternoon, knew she should eat, but she didn't want to head outside just yet.

She had woken this morning wanting to stay in the privacy of some dream, if she had dreamed.

In all this, through the years, through the chaos and all that they had lost, always the surprise of wanting, for a moment, to be alone.

Or the surprise of suddenly remembering that there was a time when all that made her miserable was simply her height. Growing up in Vientiane, she was almost always a little taller than anyone she knew, her age or older, and she was never sure how to navigate the world in her body, as though her true self was in fact inside of it somewhere, undiscovered.

Then, during the war, she would notice the ease with which people listened to her. The quickness of them following her, or stepping aside if she wanted to pass. As though they found some kind of faith in her stature. They began to call her that name, "Auntie."

Even Vang did, this childhood friend of hers who didn't remember, when they met each other again in an empty farmhouse three decades later, ninety seconds before a bombardment, how he used to tease her. On her way into the mountains, she had stopped to bring supplies for a doctor who had started a field hospital for civilians, unaware it was Vang she was bringing supplies to. "Auntie?" he said, perplexed by the name, standing in a dilapidated room with a long table. Then he smiled. She was trying to recall how long it had been. Before she could speak, he took her wrist and told her to hurry, and she had frozen, noticing for the first time, and amazed by, the wrinkles that had formed around her old friend's eyes.

Now, a lifetime later, she had settled into this new name as much as her own body.

Auntie lifted up the shirt. She was finished. Another shirt with mismatched buttons. Another with a tear in the back of it. And then she heard another noise, and through that tear in the fabric, she watched as a shadow climbed up the steps, knocked, and opened the door.

She didn't look at first to see who it was; she already knew. Then, when he didn't speak, she did look.

The man—it was an older man, thin, they were all so thin (that never failed to surprise her, too, as though each day she was determined to forget not only their hunger but their tiredness)—was out of breath but calm as he stepped in without asking, leaving the door open. Behind him, she spotted the small cluster of huts they had come upon abandoned and had been living in. That sudden intrusion of morning light.

Auntie stayed where she was. She cut the threads with her pocketknife. Then she slipped the needle back into the fabric of her cuff and folded the shirt across her lap.

"This is for the child," she said. "Do you like it?"

It was as if the man hadn't heard.

He stepped closer to her, into the hut, and said, "We found them."

•

Was it Vang who first told her that the warriors who once roamed these mountains had spirits to protect them? That each house in the villages they conquered had one, too? And that when you died, those spirits went with you?

Through the years sometimes, she would look for the wooden posts in front of a home where people placed offerings, but she had yet to encounter one, or one that had survived in the small, abandoned communities she passed through. She had seen the ruins of stone temples built for Buddhas, from both this war and ones from centuries ago— their identities unrecognizable in the maze of vines until she stepped inside, or what was once inside the remnants of a great hall or a room, the air smelling different in there, as though still carrying what it once held—she had seen all this but she had never encountered that world of spirits she and Vang used to think often about.

As children, they lived next door to each other. She would climb up to the roof of her Vientiane house to wait for him. There was a shared wall that went up to her chin, where her father, and Vang's father, had glued pieces of broken glass to the rim of it to ward off thieves from climbing over.

So she would sit back against the glass-topped wall, facing

the laundry her mother had washed hanging over a braided rope, and wait for him. This boy who would appear not long after and slide himself down against the same wall on the opposite end and begin, almost immediately, to talk.

About what? School assignments, music, the old man down below who sold poppy flowers and who fell asleep on his stool; the French café they weren't allowed to go to, but Vang went to anyway, walking by and slipping into his hand a small piece of bread left on an empty table outside; and the men who sometimes tossed him a coin from afar to run an errand, thinking he wouldn't catch it.

But Vang always did. Even then, his days and his character seemed to be formed by his hands. More than any other part of his body or sense. The touch of some part of the world. Of someone. The yearning for it. The way, when they parted, one of their parents calling from below, they would stand on their toes to look a little bit at each other, and how he would reach across the broken glass to examine her palms and fingers to make sure she was taking care of them.

All those clothes swaying on a rope. And the sound of the busy street below.

That empty sky.

•

What did they know back then? When she recalled their families and that neighborhood now, she thought of the optimism in that small corner of the country, so many of them unaware of the poverty and the lack of infrastructure in the surrounding provinces. The appearance of American aid. The North Vietnamese slipping in, wanting access to mountain roads.

She was, back then, nine at most. Vang a year younger. No older than the duration of the bombings that had finally finished so that the war existed these days, it seemed, only in name. There was the occasional raid and skirmish. And those who had survived and who had not yet fled to other countries were still being hunted.

They had caught Vang four years ago. Prany, too.

Four years.

Where were they now? What was happening to them? She didn't want to hear about it just yet.

"Let's walk," she said to the man who had come in.

She picked up the mended shirt, and together they stepped outside, walking down the hut steps they had rebuilt with stacks of wood and a pair of upside-down buckets.

It had been fifteen months since she had seen or heard a bomber approaching. She was still not yet used to the silence. Neither of them was. His name was Touby and he walked slightly behind her, to her right. He had picked up the rifle he had placed outside and slung it back over his shoulder. There was also a pistol on his belt. Tomorrow, he would cross the Mekong and hike into Thailand along with the family they had rendezvoused with in the night so that he could look again for his teenage son.

Touby had been doing this every two weeks. He had managed to get his son out a year ago, but the boy was no longer in the camp outside of Chiang Mai. Touby had lost track of him. And so far, every time, he had come back with nothing, no trace, no clue. His son could have gone to one of the dozens of nearby camps. He could have gone into Chiang Mai. Farther. Somewhere wonderful. Or it was possible he was nowhere at all. Even then, Touby needed to know.

They walked around a bomb crater in the mountain path, then past a man breaking down the wreckage of a hut to use for fire. He nodded to them, and they kept going, heading toward the clearing where they had put up the family. Out of habit, Auntie and Touby kept in the shade. The trees flanking them were no longer as verdant as they once were, but they provided shelter and, in case there were more airplanes, they were thick enough for the people here to be difficult to spot.

They relocated often, or as often as they could, but they had been situated in this abandoned village for a few months now. They ran way stations for refugees and defectors heading into Thailand. There were six of them living in the remaining huts and they took turns heading down, meeting whoever had come with enough money, which they split with the boatman, and brought them here to spend the night. Then they guided them to the river, to a bend where they had figured out the minutes between the boat patrols, just long enough for a crossing.

Their station wasn't the only one. There were several different ones scattered about, though she didn't know where; it was better that way. The separate teams communicated through couriers like Touby, who trekked across the maze of old mountain passages to send and receive a message or trade in supplies.

Auntie and Touby had been walking in silence toward the clearing, Auntie tracking the call of a bird, when she turned to him and said, "Tell me where they are now."

"Northeast," Touby said. "Close to Vietnam."

"Are they alive?"

"Yes."

"In a prison?"

"It looks like an old factory," Touby said. "They built cells inside. Fifty, perhaps. More."

"Have they been there this whole time?"

"We think so. Yes."

"What is happening to them?"

When Touby didn't respond, Auntie stopped. They were on the side of the path, near a hut in front of which two Hmong women were unpacking and sorting the food and supplies Touby had brought with him. Auntie didn't look at them, but kept her eyes fixed on Touby, who wouldn't look back at her. This man who was almost ten years older than she was suddenly, briefly, looked like a child clutching the strap of a toy gun, unsure of where to place his hands.

"Tell me," she said.

"Every day, they are brought to a room. Separately."

"Describe the room. Can you?"

"It is in the northwest corner. Ground floor. There is one high window near the ceiling. A table at the center. Steel. Two chairs on either side. Steel as well. Cuffs chained to the table. Below the table, on the floor, is a drain."

"A drain?"

"Yes."

She paused, considering everything Touby had said. "Who is in the room?"

"The interrogator. Two other men. Always behind the prisoner. Three total."

"Tell me about the interrogator."

"He served in Vietnam for a while. He came over and joined the Pathet Lao."

"So he's . . ."

"Yes, Auntie. He's good at this."

The interrogator would first be asking Prany and Vang about the CIA, she thought. Then, when they didn't know the answer—and they didn't—he would ask them about where the Hmong were. And then from there he would move on to her, and people like her. Which was what the interrogator and the Pathet Lao wanted to know all along. Vang and Prany wouldn't know that either. But that would be how she would have done it, Auntie thought, if she were interrogating them.

Four years. They had been in there already for four years.

"What has this man done to them so far?"

Touby shook his head. He didn't know, or he didn't know anyone who was sure. He said the younger one had lost the use of one of his hands. That was all he had heard.

"Prany."

"Yes. Him. It's because of the way he is working in the fields, using only one hand. They are making all of them farm and grow food. Food they aren't allowed to eat."

"Prany already knows how to farm," Auntie said. "Do you remember him?"

"I remember. Quick on the trails."

"Yes. He is very quick. Light-footed. I bet he still is. I love his smile. The only moment when his face is open. Look. I wrinkled the shirt. You never told me whether you like it."

She lifted it up for him.

"Auntie."

She had lost the thread of what she was going to say next. She shut her eyes and leaned up slightly to enter a slim path of sun. She heard that bird again, then the voices of boxes and women, and she thought of Vang's arms reaching over the wall toward her, the street noises below, and the call of Vang's father telling him to come down and study.

"Are they together?" Auntie said.

"Yes," Touby said. "They share a cell."

At least there was that. She went on, her eyes still shut: "In that room. The northwest room. Can we get to them through the drain? Or the window?"

"No. Too small. Too narrow."

"What is the material of the walls?"

"Concrete. Everywhere."

She opened her eyes. "Can we get to them?"

There wasn't time for Touby to answer. They heard a commotion coming from the clearing. Touby lifted the rifle off his shoulder and passed Auntie the pistol. The two women who had been unpacking the food fell in line with them and they headed down the path.

The family they had picked up was all standing in the clearing. The father was pulling his child toward the start of the woods while the boy's mother—the man's wife—was pulling the same boy in the opposite direction back toward the hut where Auntie had put them. Any harder and one of the parents was going to pop the child's shoulder.

The father was yelling. He said his brother was right, that this was a trick, that they weren't going anywhere but a prison, and that they were leaving now. Auntie quickly scanned the grounds. They had come with the father's brother, but he was nowhere to be seen. The mother was pulling her son and yelling at her husband to stop.

One of the women who had come with Auntie came back from inspecting the nearby hut and said into Auntie's ear that the brother was gone. Then she moved slowly in a circle on Auntie's left, sideways, right foot past her left. Touby was slowly moving in the opposite direction, rifle raised, away from the man, but also looking for a clear shot if it came to that. Noticing the rifle, the boy, perhaps seven, in the middle of all this, who had been silent the whole time, immobile and confused and in pain from the pulling, began to cry.

Auntie, who had not lifted her pistol, stepped forward. In

that moment, the mother's grip on her son slipped—*Good*, Auntie thought—and the boy was pulled toward his father. Then the father spun the boy around in front of him and brought his arms, viselike, around the boy's head and began stepping back.

Auntie had often seen this, a man's illogical, panic-driven decision, if one were to call it that, to threaten strangers with the remote possibility of harming what he cherished the most. It was an ineffable curiosity. What wasn't was that the child's face was now turning a darker color as his ankles dragged along the dirt, backward.

Ten steps before they were in the woods.

"I'm better than some trick," the father yelled.

"I know it," Auntie said. Then, with her arms spread, she lowered her pistol onto the ground. She told the others to stop. She kept stepping forward, slowly, and this time the father didn't step back, but stayed where he was. She could hear the mother weeping somewhere behind her. She wanted to hear that bird one more time.

"We aren't forcing you to stay," Auntie said. "You can go. You can go anywhere you'd like. This isn't a trick. But please. Please. Leave the child alone."

"I'm better than all of you," the father said.

"Yes, you are."

"Better than all of this. What is this exactly? Charity? Does my losing everything make you feel better? Look at yourselves. You are living like thieves. I'm no coward. I don't run away."

Auntie, still stepping closer to him, said, "Look down at what you are doing to your child."

He had not moved. Auntie was standing in front of him now. With her arms still spread out, she lowered herself onto her knees.

"I'm not a coward," the father said. "I don't run away."

And then he paused and finally looked down. The boy's face had gone a bright dark. There was snot dripping down his nose onto his father's forearm. Auntie held her breath. With her middle finger she felt for the needle in her shirt cuff. She exhaled and breathed again. Then she changed her mind, flicked open her pocketknife with her thumb, reached around the man's legs, and sliced his calf quickly, and deeply.

It happened so fast the man didn't realize at first if anything had, in fact, happened. He reacted to it as though a bird had passed low against his legs, its wing brushing him, but in that moment, as his expression held that surprise, almost like wonder, he released the boy, and at once Touby and the woman rushed forward and pinned the father down to the ground.

Auntie checked on the boy. She found his pulse as the

color of his face returned. She left him to the mother and grabbed the shirt with the new buttons she had dropped and tore it into strips. Then she moved to the man whose leg was bleeding heavily, the pant leg dark and damp, the ground below, too.

"It looks worse than it is," she said, tying his calf up. "It's just a flesh wound. You'll be fine."

The father, who had remained lying on the ground, had become impossibly quiet. There was nothing in his eyes. Kneeling over him, Auntie reached for his shoulder and held him like this, briefly.

"I promise," Auntie said. "I will get you across."

Then she stood and walked away from the clearing. She walked back down the path toward the boxes that were half unpacked and stood among them, catching her breath. She folded her knife, shut her eyes, and leaned into the morning light again.

What was it that she had been thinking of? Something Vang had said years ago. How sometimes it was necessary to distract a patient from their pain with another, smaller, more focused pain.

She stepped into the sun. She was back by the rooftop wall again. The street noises and the poppy flowers. Vang standing up and reaching over. This future doctor who used to say that in another life, if he were an orphan, he would be a concert pianist. That she could be his violinist, which always made her laugh; she knew no instruments.

Just the voice of that young boy as the colors of the broken glass on top of the wall played against his wrists.

•

Auntie was startled awake sometime in the middle of the night. She reached for her pistol and then in the silence of the hut recognized that it had been the push of a dream. Her throat was raw; she was starving. When a shadow passed outside the door, she got up to find Touby sitting on one of the bucket steps, still carrying his rifle.

"Aren't you on shift?" she said.

He was supposed to be making his rounds. They took turns with that, too. She had no idea what time it was, but the moon was full and everything around them was clear. It was cooler, almost cold tonight, and she thought perhaps that was why his hand was trembling, though when she reached for the tin cup he was holding, she saw that he was warm.

"You didn't have to do that," he said.

She took the cup and she sat with him.

"Do what?"

"Cut him."

"Your bullet would have been worse," she said, but he didn't go on.

Auntie drank what was left in the cup. It was tea that had come in with the shipment. Warm tea.

"Did I do anything in my sleep?" she said. "Could you hear?"

He didn't answer. The shadow of some small animal—how lovely it was to see an animal—scurried across the front of the hut into the woods. Otherwise, there was again that silence.

"I always wondered if I did. Whether I move or say something while I dream. My body here and my mind somewhere else. Whether that is what startles me awake. Myself."

"I don't think I can do this anymore," Touby said.

He was staring out at the moonlight on the ground. She thought he was thinking of his son, but she wondered if it was something else entirely. They had been working together for longer, it seemed, than she had lived next door to Vang. She could no longer imagine the days without him, though she knew of course that there would eventually be such days.

"You did well today," Auntie said. "The food. The supplies. You did really well. Now finish your shift. And leave tomorrow. Go find your son. Tell him whatever it is he needs to hear and whatever it is you need to say. Then come back."

She gave him the cup and headed down the path they had been on earlier. She passed a stack of firewood and the bomb crater where there was a faint reflection at the bottom of it. And then she walked past the hut where the two Hmong women were staying, where the boxes had been unpacked, the food and the supplies stored away.

In the day's disturbance, she had forgotten to pick up the rest of the shirt. No one else had either. It was still there in the clearing, near the border to the woods, a pale mound, like moss, on top of the tree stump where she had thrown it. Nearby, the family was asleep in the hut. She almost checked in on them but crossed the clearing instead, leaving the shirt where it was, and entered the woods. She went far enough so that she could see the valley and, in the clear night, the ruin of an abandoned landscape far below.

She scanned the distance, catching the occasional sweep of a patrol light on a far road. When the light went away, she went back to the shirt, unwearable now, and cut off all of its buttons, which she returned to her pouch. Then, using what was left of the shirt, she wiped the surface of the tree stump, remembering the miracle of having a chicken one day, years ago, and how she had beheaded it, plucked its feathers, and gutted it. And how she had found Prany there the next day, sitting on the ground, his head on that same stump, looking up. How much that had stilled her.

She thought of that northwest room again.

He and Vang had arrived together one day at her camp, unexpectedly. She had been certain that they had already fled to France. When she saw Vang, she had rushed to him, fighting, for an instant, the joy that he hadn't. He and Prany had missed their helicopter. For months at that camp, they didn't speak. And for months, she didn't know why. Then she did. Vang waking her in the middle of the night in the hut they shared, his hand pressed over her mouth as he told her to shut up, to stop talking in her sleep. And then, as quickly as a rainstorm, the doctor told her about the accident, about how Prany had turned around, ignoring the pleas of the people already in the helicopter, and gone back for them. Then Vang mentioned Prany's sister, began to hyperventilate, and wept.

It was sometime after this that he and Prany began to talk again. She didn't know the reason for it. If there was a reason. Perhaps in their exhaustion and hunger and their constant hiding, they had erased themselves so completely they had become strangers meeting for the first time.

But she found them one day arguing over who could better carry the supplies a courier had smuggled in. For a while, she walked with them on the narrow but bright mountain road that would lead them to the community that had temporarily become theirs. They were alone, the three of them. Perhaps for the first time. The sky was quiet. As she watched the trees above them sway, she almost forgot where they were and what they were doing. Vang's glasses slipped down his nose, and before she could say something, Prany reached over and used his knuckle to push them back up.

•

Before dawn, they guided the family down to the Mekong River. Auntie, one of the Hmong women, and Touby. Auntie was in the back and Touby led. Touby was carrying a rucksack with a half day's worth of supplies for himself and the family. After the crossing, they would have to hike for two hours to the Thai border, where someone would be waiting for them.

In that paling dark, it took an hour for them to descend the mountain. When they could hear the current of the river, they stopped. They stayed in the forest off the path until a patrol boat sped by, the light panning the banks. As soon as it rounded the bend, they left the shelter of the trees, hurrying to the water, where an old man was waiting for them behind a wall of branches set up on the bank, cupping his cigarette so that the glow of it wasn't visible.

"Five minutes," he said.

They all helped remove the branches to reveal the motorized raft that looked ancient, a portion of it made up of rusty shell casings strapped together.

"Any day this will go," Auntie said in a whisper to him, and he took a drag and said in a whisper back, "Let's hope not today, then. Four minutes."

The family got on first. The father, his leg bandaged, looked back at her once, briefly, and nodded. Then Touby turned to her and smiled.

"Not once," he said. "Not once have you gone across. And not once, not all this time, have you ever told me your name."

Auntie tapped her thigh. "You never asked," she said.

Touby laughed quietly, tracking the current of the dark, wide river. In the predawn, he was a shadow in her periphery.

"Three minutes," the boatman said.

"I'll tell you the next time we see each other," Auntie said.

They had not spoken about the night before and she knew they wouldn't. They had not spoken further about that northwest corner room either. She watched as Touby climbed down the bank and stepped on. As soon as he did, the boatman pushed the raft away with a pole and started the motor.

Two minutes.

The raft swayed from the weight of the passengers, slow

to move, but found its balance and soon they were crossing. It moved more quickly than she expected it to. It always did. Yet she wished in that moment that there was a drain on the bottom of the river. That all that water would go so that they could simply walk. It was a silly thought, a child's thought, but watching the raft head out farther, she wished it anyway. A drain.

They were already approaching the far bank when one of the shell casings loosened and the raft tipped, deep enough so that one end dipped into the water, and she watched as Touby, who was closest to the edge, began to lose his balance and fall. She stepped down into the river, holding her breath, but just then the father reached for Touby's rucksack and held him.

The raft tilted back up, and then they were across.

"Forty seconds," the woman behind Auntie said.

Together they watched as everyone scrambled to collect the branches on the other side and hide the boat and themselves. Then, on this side of the bank, the woman and Auntie did the same, lowering themselves onto the ground. The cool earth on her chest.

They heard the patrol rounding the bend. The light panning over them. She waited for the engine noise to fade and then, slowly, carefully, they began to remove the branches that were covering them.

She turned to the woman and said, "Set up a meeting."

She meant with the others who were scattered across these mountains, hiding.

The woman wondered if it was too dangerous, but Auntie pretended not to hear.

"Is this about the doctor?" the woman said.

It was always about the doctor, she almost said, and was briefly convinced that she had in fact said this, though she wasn't sure why. It wasn't something she believed—had ever thought about until now—and yet the words skipped across inside her like a flat stone over the river.

The sun was starting to crest the high opposite ridge, clarifying their surroundings. The woman told her they should go, that the others had already gone. All they could hear was the rush of the current now.

Three minutes.

Auntie glanced across and then wiped the dirt from her trousers, noticing for the first time the pinprick of dried blood near her pocket from yesterday.

PRANY

(1977)

They were released.

For the first time in seven years, they stood outside in the courtyard of the reeducation center. They looked across at the gate. They remembered none of this. The flagpole and the towers. The cameras. Prany counted the sentries in the towers. *Six.* He heard the rattle of keys as the guard behind him, wearing a green uniform, undid his handcuffs. Then the guard undid Vang's. They rubbed their free wrists. Vang made fists with his hands.

Prany dug the soles of his new shoes into the dirt. He watched Vang's hands and then he turned to see the building from where they had exited. It was an old factory. The same color stone as the walls. The flag flapped in the wind. The sun on him. All that blue sky. His neck was stiff. He knew that if they were forced to run right now, his legs might buckle. Not because he was weak, but because in this moment, in the new environment, out in the open, his entire body felt uncertain.

It was early. A different guard wearing a short-brimmed hat stepped out from the balcony above them and lit a cigarette. A rifle was slung behind him. His figure tall against the sky. He tapped his cigarette and the ash fell, already cold by the time it hit Prany's shoulders. The guard tried again, aiming at Prany's face.

Prany pretended not to notice. He couldn't stop looking at the sky. From inside came the faint noise of an announcement on the loudspeakers. Then he caught the sounds that had kept them company through the years: the hum of the electrical wires outside the cells, the footsteps in the small rear yard where they were able to play a bit of soccer, and during the monsoons feel the rain on them.

The birds. He remembered the shock of hearing one, unable to recall the last time he had. It was almost enough to get him through the week. He had once stopped in the field where he had been forced to work, listening to it, not caring that in ten seconds he would be punished for stopping. Then the desire to see the bird had driven him insane.

Someone was playing soccer now. He caught the sound of a ball bouncing, waited for another. An hour ago, they had signed documents pledging loyalty to this country. They had been brought to a concrete room where there was a long, wooden desk and two chairs across from each other. A portrait of the prime minister was hanging on the wall. Then a man they had never seen before, wearing an ill-fitting suit, came in, sat on the chair below the portrait, and gestured for Prany to take the other.

Prany was unused to the grip of a pen. He wrote slowly, watching the ink appear and bleed, forming his name. A part of him was stunned he still knew how to write it. He had never learned how to read or to write, had hardly ever considered language as something visible, but from Vang they had learned how to write their names one night at the farmhouse, all of them unable to sleep. Vang by a desk with three legs, the other built of books, and the three of them taking turns writing on a damp page in his notebook, in candlelight, the ink smearing as they ignored the sound of the distant bombers.

Years after that night, in their cell one day, he wondered out loud where the notebook was, and Vang, pausing, replied, "I never had a notebook."

That was the first time Prany began to doubt his memories.

In the room, Prany asked the official in the suit across from him what day it was. The official seemed surprised.

They knew months and years. They didn't trust days.

The officer said, "Today is Wednesday, the second of February, 1977."

It suddenly occurred to Prany he couldn't recall how his sister wrote her name, would not have been able to identify her handwriting among a thousand others.

"When did I come in?" Prany said.

The guard behind him reached for Prany's neck and slammed him down against the desk. Prany clutched the pen. Immediately, his nose began to bleed. His nose often bled. He snorted it up as hard as he could and swallowed his blood and wiped his lips with his tongue. The official was looking at him as though Prany had asked him whether he owned sheep.

"You came in on the tenth of January, 1970. Both of you did. You were at one of those decrepit mountain camps. All of you, how many were there? One hundred? Hiding like mice in your huts with your ten bullets and rusty rainwater. You couldn't even farm. So malnourished you were probably dying and didn't know it. All that, because of what? You lost. We are not animals. We would have taken care of you. We *did* take care of you."

Behind him, Vang, silent, was leaning against the wall beside the guard.

"We're approaching the next decade," Prany said.

"Yes. Quite."

"How's it going so far?"

From behind, he heard the guard step toward him again, but the official waved him away. The man took off his glasses and cleaned them slowly, looking across at Vang, whose own glasses were covered in so many scratches he could hardly see through them.

"A new decade for you, too," the man said. "Your age."

"That's right. A new decade for me."

"That's lovely," the man said. "A fresh start."

"Yes," Prany said. "A fresh start."

"How many men are given that in life? It is a gift. To start again. To have that chance. You are now a member of this society, men of this society, both of you, and you get to contribute to its success. What a gift."

Only then did the man reach across and take back the pen. It was as though he were waiting to see what Prany would do with it. Prany had done nothing. He watched the man tap it on the edge of the desk and consider Prany. *Tap, tap, tap.*

He then took out a file and confirmed their relocation and new postings at a village in Luang Prabang. From a sheet he read to them that they would report to the administrative office tonight. There was a temporary room in a house that they could stay in for the week. It had all been arranged. This was also a great gift for them: to be together, given that they were not related. Others were not so lucky, he said.

"As you have learned, our country is rich in natural resources and we should develop them. Under the old regime we were not working hard enough, yes? How could we under such oppression and disorder? So dysfunctional were we over the years, corrupted by and reliant on the Japanese, the French, the Americans. All these people always crossing our borders, claiming to want to help us. Liberate us. But now, here, all of us, look at us now. We broke that cycle. We freed you. We taught you how to be self-sufficient. We taught you how to grow food if you didn't know how. We taught you how to build fish ponds. To raise pigs and chickens. You worked this land. Every day, you worked this land. This center, as far back as it goes, was your land. You helped us, and you helped yourselves. It is all wonderful. Now you will be self-sufficient. You will use all this knowledge to help your village. And then your village will help others. You will, together, collectively, be hardworking and clean and pure. You will prosper from your education these past years, and you will think on this day as the first in your new life and be grateful to us."

"You're very generous today," Prany said, and this time the man leaned across and gripped Prany's left hand, crushing the fingers hard, pulling him across the desk. Prany stifled a scream.

"The party and government's intelligence is clear and bright," the official said. "All praise, all praise, all praise."

Vang quickly repeated the words and then, after a pause, Prany, breathing between his teeth, said them, too: "The party and government's intelligence is clear and bright: all praise, all praise, all praise."

The official let go. For the first time, he addressed Vang: "I am actually feeling quite generous today. But you'll have to keep an eye on this one. In fact, if he gets into any trouble, it's you we'll come for, yes? Do you understand? He's your responsibility now."

The official looked down at the file.

"Doctor," he said. "Yes. Quite. Sorry, no doctor postings available."

He chuckled and gave them their new papers. He also slid over a set of clothes for them that smelled harshly of chemicals. Then the official stood, congratulating them on their reeducation, and wished the two of them good health, good work, and long, peaceful lives.

Now, in the courtyard, a van pulled up. The guard on the balcony went inside. Prany held on to a head cushion and climbed up after Vang did. The windows had been blacked out. The divide between their seats and the front had been walled up as well, so that they were blind as they drove across the courtyard, the van bouncing slightly as they left through the gate.

Without turning, Vang spoke to Prany softly, the way they were used to doing. He was whispering in French. On the second day, using a hammer, they had broken the bones of the doctor's fingers first, wanting names of CIA officers. Wanting the location of Hmong fighters. And a woman they called "Auntie." Then they broke Prany's fingers.

Vang's recovered. Prany lost the use of his left hand.

"The dates," Vang said. "In that room. Why did you want to know the dates?"

The van bounced again as they turned onto a smoother road. The driver sped. In the dark, Prany could hear only the air. He watched the quick shadows in the thin space along the bottom of the side door. He had forgotten about speed. The speed of a vehicle. He grew light-headed again. He fought it by breathing deeply.

In the prison, after the first three years, they had mostly left Prany alone, but they had kept returning to Vang. They called him the pretty doctor. The men would lift him by his arms and drag him down the hall, barefoot, to where the interrogator was waiting for him, and he would be gone for an hour. Prany couldn't hear him. He couldn't hear anything. He counted the seconds to distract himself and to time how long he was alone. In that hour, it was the complete silence that terrified them.

Vang asked him again. "Why did you want to know the dates?"

Prany said that he wanted to hear someone other than themselves say it out loud. The months, the years. He asked if Vang understood. This doctor, whom he had now known for a decade and who had kept practicing French with him in the cell as a thread of sanity.

Vang, whom he would never see again after today.

"Stay focused," Vang said. "We're out."

The doctor mimed punching the ceiling a few times, his arms like pistons, restless as they sped across the smoothness of a paved highway. The wind grew louder. The engine.

Seven years. Prany was twenty-five. Vang was almost forty.

They had no idea where they were.

•

They were dropped off at a bus station near Vang Vieng. It didn't matter anymore, but he had timed how long they had been in the van and wondered if they had been kept somewhere in the north, near the Chinese border.

There was a time when Prany used to spend all day attempting to orient himself by the shape of a far slope, the temperature during the colder months. The wind and the weather, or the flight path of a bird—*a bird*! This need for a compass. The delirium of it. He would have offered his other hand to simply know.

When the van door opened, unaccustomed to the daylight, Prany was still unsure of where he was, whether he was in fact still in Laos. He almost wept. It wasn't because he recognized the bus station. He had never seen it before. It was simply because they hadn't been taken back, that the building was different from the buildings of the prison.

And because they were still in Laos.

"Take the first bus," the guard in the passenger seat said. "Wait at the bench. Good health." And then the van drove away, leaving the two of them in front of the station, which appeared empty.

Vang knelt to retie his shoes. They had been given matching clothes—white shirts, gray trousers, and black shoes—and they were getting used to them, the feel of them, that smell, the shapes. Whose clothes were they wearing? In first imagining and then planning this day, they had been uncertain about the clothes. To them it was a miracle that they had been given anything at all.

They were about two hundred kilometers southwest of Phonsavan. Closer to Vientiane. They lifted their hands for shade, squinting against the brightness as they walked around to the back of the station. In a dirt yard was the shell of what had been a school bus, rusted, propped up on bricks. Behind it, two small billboards that had probably been intended for the roadside were stacked against the wall: the first was an illustration of an elephant carrying felled logs through a forest; the other depicted a woman repairing a chair.

No one came. But Vang kept a lookout as Prany opened the lid of a trash container. He didn't spot the box at first. He saw only the garbage and some rotten fruit and rice and his heart began to beat quickly as he wondered if something had happened. If something had gone wrong.

But it was there, farther below: the black shoe box, like they were promised.

He flipped it open. Inside, there was a thick envelope of money and a small hunting knife, the blade folded into the metal handle. A stray dog appeared, sniffing their shoes, his nose following the scent of the garbage. Prany reached into the garbage container again and tossed the dog a handful of the fruit and rice. Then he passed the money and the knife to Vang and together they returned to the front of the station and waited.

They waited standing in the quiet, with a mountain range in the east and a village to the north, a small collection of rooftops by the river. They were distracted by the vast emptiness. There were no buses, no one on the road. There was only the mountain. The distance.

Then, from the road, an old man appeared, crossing the lot and sitting on the bench near the front entrance of the station. He was wearing similar clothes as them, and they waited to see if he would try to speak to them, but he didn't. He lifted up his sleeve as though he had a watch and scratched a knuckle in a way that made Prany suddenly remember a girl he had met in a southern town. He had convinced her to ride a rickshaw he had stolen for an hour to try to make some money. This was during a lull in the fighting during a heavy, rainy season. Her profile in the rearview and the scent of her in the back as she kept reaching over his shoulder, her money grazing his ear as she told him to keep going.

Where did they go? Prany tried to remember. He and Vang hadn't moved from the station entrance. He was tired. They were both so tired. Shy of the new landscape. This new world. Still afraid. The way the feeling was there like a contrail as they kept gazing out at the horizontal distance. How nothing came up from behind the ridgeline, how in five minutes nothing in the landscape had altered. How there was no sound other than the wind. The gait of the dog and the dust.

"Shall we walk?" Prany said.

They could. In their plan, they had talked about saving their energy, but it wasn't far. Prany suddenly wanted to walk forever. He thought he could. He paced a little. He could feel his heart. Together, they tracked a bird in the air. How many birds did they end up watching? He had witnessed the doctor grow older. Gray was starting in his hair. In his memory of the man, there was only this face now, not the one that would lean so close to the keyboard of the piano that they thought he was going to disappear into it.

Prany remembered now. Eventually, he took the girl to a ceremony a relative of hers was hosting. She got out without looking at him and then, to his surprise, took his wrist and made him follow her up a hill. They entered a landscape he had never seen: a high field, unbroken by the war, domed in suspended candlelit lanterns hanging from poles. It was as though he had stumbled upon that other world the shamans claimed they had access to. There was a small crowd and the shaman was standing at the center. The girl he had driven took the string the crowd gave her and bound her wrist and then bound the rest of the string to Prany's. They were all bound, the entire crowd. And then they approached the shaman, who flung the smoke of incense over them.

He came back never knowing what they were celebrating or wishing for, just that they had been bound, him with those strangers and the girl, and that they had been blessed. Still in the echo of it as Alisak and Noi slept by a river. He had stopped on the way and bought as many pears from a peddler as he could carry, the fruit spilling from his arms. They never noticed he was gone. Only the new scent on him, the incense and the girl's perfume of herbs and flowers.

A car appeared, approaching the bus station. They tracked

it like the bird as it approached, slowed, and turned in. The old man on the bench ignored it. Other than the van that had dropped them off, it was the first vehicle they had seen. They checked the road one last time for any sign of the bus they had been ordered to take, but nothing else appeared over the ridge.

The window rolled down. "Faster to ride with me," the driver said. He nodded and gestured for them to come in. He was wearing sunglasses. They had slid down his nose and he looked first at Vang and then at Prany, who brought his arms behind him.

It was a taxi. Or some version of one; there were no signs. There were strips of duct tape across the passenger seat and a jug of water on the floor. They checked as quickly and discreetly as possible—what he was wearing, the dash, the back seat—for any clue that he might be an official or Pathet Lao, but couldn't find any.

So Prany named an inn on the western side of a reservoir. It wasn't very far, perhaps four kilometers south. He asked the driver if he could take them there.

"I know it," the driver said, and named a price.

They didn't argue with him. They got in, and then they were heading south. They stayed silent, staring out the windows. Prany kept waiting to get used to the speed of a vehicle. The speed of the world passing. The undulating shapes of the hills. An abandoned farm and what looked like a new cement factory. There were bomb craters in fields that hadn't yet been filled and a roadside restaurant, the windows and the door all gone.

The driver was eyeing them through the rearview.

"What time is it?" Vang said.

"What?"

"The time." Vang lifted his wrist.

"Noon," the driver said.

Vang grinned. It had been years since he had asked for the time and someone had answered him. He leaned forward and asked if they could hear music. The driver laughed, pressed a button on the radio. All they could hear was static.

"You're not from here," he said.

They approached the boundary of the massive reservoir that seemed to them an inland ocean. It was impossible to see the far bank. The taxi followed the road that ran along the reservoir's western side, passing islands, some of them with old structures. A blue ferryboat with no passengers cut across the water. Then, just as quickly, they drove away from the reservoir and entered a forest. Soon, a sign for the inn appeared, and the driver turned onto an unpaved road that they followed for less than a kilometer until it opened out onto a round courtyard.

The building was on the far end. It was a wide, two-story structure with fading red paint and dark window shutters. There were some plants and a copper sculpture of a fish at the center of the courtyard, so oxidized they were unsure what it was at first, the fish in midair, as though caught and being reeled in.

"So then, where are you from?" the driver said, pulling up to the front.

They had practiced this.

"Phonsavan," Prany said.

They had practiced this every day for years, but in that moment he didn't say what he was supposed to say. Suddenly, those years collapsed, and he felt as though he were falling. It was too late now. He knew Vang was avoiding looking at him. It would be the one mistake Prany would think of, not at this moment, but one day months from now, leaping out of a van and running.

"I have a cousin in Phonsavan," the driver said. "Good restaurant. You must know it, yes? Best food in the town."

He named the restaurant. He said, "Survived the war, the restaurant," and Vang said, "Yes. Great," and took out double the amount the driver had asked for. The driver paused, trying to hide his surprise. Then he pushed up his sunglasses and slipped the money into his back pocket.

"I can wait," the driver said. "If you have somewhere else to go."

They shook their heads, opened the door, and got out.

"You tell my cousin I drove you today, yes? When you get back. You're on a trip, yes? But tell him when you get back."

They waited for him to drive back down the unpaved road through the forest. "Don't worry," Vang said, and reached for the copper fish, wanting to touch it, but changed his mind.

They headed in. The brief burst of a ceiling fan spinning above them. There was another fish in the small lobby, this one made of gold and standing on a pedestal. It was gleaming. The floors, too. Above them hung a chandelier. They caught the scent of flowers. The sound of trickling water. It was the most opulence they had encountered since the farmhouse, and they didn't move, suddenly distracted by it all until a young man standing behind the reception counter called to them and smiled.

It wasn't him.

Behind the receptionist, on the wall, were room numbers and large hooks for the keys. All the keys were hanging on their hooks. Prany and Vang glanced at each other and then they asked if there was a room available.

From somewhere down the hall came faint music. A slow ballad Prany thought he recognized.

"Only one?" the receptionist said, continuing to smile, looking at Prany and then Vang.

"Yes."

The receptionist said if they wanted two separate rooms he could offer them a discount.

"Are we the only guests?" Vang said.

"Two rooms," the receptionist said, ignoring him. "It might be more comfortable that way. And a discount."

"Only one," they said.

The receptionist regarded them, their clothes. He asked for identification.

This was the moment they had been curious about. They had no identification. They had their papers but they were supposed to be on a bus crossing the country by now. They opened the envelope and passed a handful of money over to him and said they had forgotten to bring their papers, that they were very tired from a long trip, that they were teachers at a school, and they were heading back home to Vientiane and wanted only to spend the night. They handed him another stack of money to be safe.

Whatever the receptionist was considering was unreadable. They waited, holding their breaths. The sound of trickling water seemed to grow louder. Then the young man took the money and selected a key from the wall. As he slid it across the counter, he asked if they needed help with their luggage. They said no. He smiled again. There were maps on the counter of the area if they wanted to take a walk. There were also flyers promoting "self-sustainability" with brightly colored illustrations of farms and lush grass.

They asked if there was a restaurant, and the receptionist pointed down a hall. Then he looked around, leaned forward, and said, quietly, "Please. No sex stuff, okay?"

They didn't know how to respond to that.

"Okay," Vang said, and they went to the restaurant.

There were five tables in the room. They sat in the corner by a window with a view of a small garden. They had the restaurant to themselves. Prany placed his hands on the tablecloth, feeling the texture of it. Outside, a child wandered the garden path, shouting on occasion at someone they couldn't see and pointing at the soil. They had seen so few people today, but it was still unbelievable to Prany to be seeing someone other than those they had seen for years. To see them unharmed. Unbelievable to be seeing different clothes. To be seeing a child.

The receptionist appeared by their table, this time wearing an apron. He fumbled with a notebook and wet the tip of his pen with his tongue. They asked what the kitchen was serving, and he pointed behind him at a chalkboard on the wall. There were two things. Vegetables and rice. And, to their surprise, meat and rice. In the camp, they had never seen the animals they had raised after they had brought them across the fields to be slaughtered. The way all the animals' gaits changed as though they understood that something different was about to occur, and Prany unable to look into their eyes.

They ordered four servings of each. The young man hesitated, wondering if he had misheard, so they said it again: four of the vegetables and rice, and four of the meat and rice. Then they asked what kind of drinks, and they ordered everything he listed. Sodas, beer. They asked if there was anything else in the kitchen that wasn't on the menu. The receptionist had stopped writing. He said they probably had some papaya and some kaipen, and so they ordered all of that, too. They took out the envelope and gave him another stack of money. He pocketed the bills without looking at them and hurried away. They would do everything to get the manager's attention.

Outside, the child trampled a plant. Not long after, a young woman appeared in the garden and knelt by the ruined plant and began to salvage as much of it as she could. She was perhaps Prany's age and wearing slippers. Prany watched as she rolled up her sleeves to collect the dirt that had fallen on the stones of the path and carried it back over into the garden.

Over and over she did this, somehow avoiding getting dirt on her clothes or even on her slippers.

Prany studied her profile. Her patience. Her resemblance to the man they were looking for. There was no mention of a family. Did it matter? It didn't to him. He glanced at Vang, but the doctor was looking down at the section of the floor between his feet and rapidly tapping his chest with his fingers. Prany returned to the woman out the window: she brushed the dirt from her hands and left, ducking under the low branches of two trees.

Where was the food?

As the minutes passed, Vang still tapping his chest, Prany began to wonder if this was all a hallucination. That these last years of planning had been a hallucination. That any moment now someone would appear and clap or begin to laugh, maybe Auntie herself would appear, and then the lights would go out and the daylight would vanish. That the woman and the child outside and this inn would vanish. That the loudspeakers would blare, rattling their eardrums like a detonation, and it would turn out that they hadn't left the prison at all, and this was another one of the guards' games. And that the man who had interrogated them for years was waiting for them in that same room that had turned Vang so quiet.

For a moment, this seemed possible.

But the food arrived. All the food arrived. They could smell it everywhere now. It was everywhere. They leaned over the table and ate. At first, they ate with shyness and then almost violently. It was dry and not very warm; the meat was tough and the rice was almost raw, but they tasted flavors they had forgotten existed and ones they had thought of so often that Vang began to cry silently. He wiped his eyes and kept eating. They didn't speak. They drank their beers and ate and opened the colorful bottles of Fantas and drank them, too, shocked by the sudden sugar, some of it spilling from their mouths onto their shirts. They kept eating and drinking. They ignored the receptionist watching them from the kitchen door. No one else came into the restaurant. They ordered more Fantas and beer and one more dish.

When the receptionist came back again, Prany asked how the inn had meat, had all of this. They slid him more money, and Prany gestured out to the garden and the lobby.

"The manager," the receptionist said. "He knows people."

"Where is he?" Vang said.

"He's a good man. He takes care of us. My family. He's a good man."

They slid him more money.

"He hasn't come in yet."

"When will he come in?"

"Soon," he said.

"Tell him to come see us, yes?" Vang said.

"Is there a problem? He's a good man."

"No problem."

They went to the room. They had trouble finding theirs, uncertain of how the numbers on the doors proceeded, but then they found the stairs and went up. They had been given a corner room on the second floor. The hallway smelled of damp wood. Prany took the key and tried the lock but it wouldn't turn. He tried again. They thought they heard footsteps and stopped, but no one came. Prany passed the key to Vang. The key turned. They stepped inside.

There were two Western-style double beds. Red mattress covers. A brochure, trifolded and standing up. Vang laughed softly. *Beds!* They turned on the light in the bathroom and saw the folded towels and the toilet. A shower. Then they froze at their reflections in the mirror, their similar clothes, their gauntness, the deep hollows of their cheekbones, and their broken posture. Their age. They stood in silence, avoiding looking at each other through the mirror. They were just bones and old, older.

They returned to the beds. Prany sat on the edge of the one closest to the window, where there was a view of the back of the inn, the paths, the hills. He waited for the child and the mother, but they didn't appear.

They took off their clothes and folded them carefully on top of the dresser. Prany's working papers slipped from the pocket of his trousers and he knelt to examine them. He didn't know what all the words meant. He tore the papers up, Vang's too, and flushed them down the toilet. He grabbed a towel like Vang had, wrapped himself in it, and went over to the bed. The room was small, but to them it was a palace. He thought he would walk around because he could, but like Vang, he ended up staying there on the bed as though not wanting to leave the borders of it.

He reached over the space between the beds and held Vang's hand. "What if he doesn't come?"

"He'll come," Vang said.

"But if he doesn't?"

Vang didn't answer. Prany kept holding him. He watched as the doctor breathed as slowly as he could. His own heart was pounding, but he focused on Vang's breathing the way they had practiced, matching his, and as they waited, it was as though he were falling and floating somewhere terribly far and deep and vast. He thought of Noi and the pears he had dropped that had rolled down the banks of the river, the way he had chased after them, and he thought of how he had bashed his head against the wall one day in the cell, over and over again, until Vang woke, pinned him down, and held him.

He remembered the soothing hum of a song coming deep within the doctor's chest as Vang tried to stop the bleeding with his shirt. Then a joke Vang made about how, in a cell, it was impossible for him to misplace his glasses.

He saw that hall of mirrors in the farmhouse and the woman who had kept wanting to get up, forgetting she had lost the use of her legs. The way they had left her and so many others there, on that last day, unable to move them as they had fled.

That day so many years ago, after leaving the farmhouse and arriving at the schoolyard alone, a helicopter already there, he had gone back for them. Alisak and Noi, the nurse and Vang. He had driven back across the Plain of Jars, seeing smoke rising from a field. A farmer waving a pale shirt, indicating to him someone was alive.

Prany only found Vang. By then, the helicopters had already gone. In their desperation, they had driven across the country, all the way toward the Mekong.

He thought of the papers he had just torn up, floating in the toilet water. He imagined the life that had been given to them this morning and understood it would not have been all that bad. He felt the rhythm of going to work every day and helping a village grow food. It seemed good; it seemed okay. It was something he could have done. He knew how. He could do things like that now. He could help a village and a village could help other villages. Maybe he should. Maybe the reeducation center had been right and they had helped him. Maybe what was waiting for them was wonderful. He let go of Vang, their arms falling.

Prany woke to footsteps. The sudden knock that snuck into him and rattled his teeth. He crossed the room and peered into the eyehole.

There he was. They had imagined this day for so long, but as he opened the door, they forgot to envision that the man standing in the hall by their room entrance was now, like them, older. Much older. That the man who had been their interrogator when they had arrived, the man who had used a hammer on their fingers and who had continued to torture them, who had continued to torture Vang, had aged. His hair was thinner and gray. He had gained weight around his waist and was wearing a collared short-sleeved shirt with a tiny horse embroidered on it. He seemed, simply, like an old father. Someone healthy and at peace.

It was clear the interrogator didn't recognize them. They were sure he wouldn't have. What had they been to him? So little. They had been so little. Information they didn't have. It took them a year to discover where he had gone, that he had retired and had inherited this inn from an uncle.

"I'm the manager of this establishment," he said. "I wanted to personally welcome you to the Vientiane Prefecture, the most beautiful place here in Laos, the most beautiful place in the world. All praise, all praise, all praise."

"All praise, all praise, all praise," they said.

The interrogator looked over Prany's shoulder at Vang. If he was disturbed that they were only in their towels he hid it. He said, "Please let me know if there's anything you need, and I will personally assist you."

Prany opened the door farther. He apologized for their appearance. He said they had stained their clothes and were waiting for them to dry. He gestured for the manager to come in and offered him a chair by a small table in the corner. The interrogator stayed where he was, holding the bottle of whiskey he had brought with him. He offered it to them, but they declined. He wiped his brow with a handkerchief. His eyes stayed on Vang, who was by the window, and they waited to see if some recognition came.

The manager shut the door behind him and locked it. He opened the whiskey and drank it himself. He asked where they were from. Whether they were enjoying their stay. He said he catered mostly to foreign diplomats and that it was rare to have guests of such means who weren't here officially. That it was quite the honor for him. That he heard they were teachers, but he knew that was not true, though they need not worry, he was most discreet.

Then, more quietly, he asked if they needed entertainment. He said they looked like men who wanted to have some fun. He said, "You like the young entertainment? I know the young entertainment." He wiped his mouth with the back of his hand and said again that he was most discreet. That he knew the best and the youngest. Fresh like the best fruit.

"Fresh like the best fruit," Vang said.

Before the interrogator could say anything else, Prany and Vang stepped toward him, grabbed his arms and his head, and threw him down against the table so that his body was folded over the edge. They twisted his chin up, shoved a small towel into his mouth, lifted him back up, and slammed him down again. They pulled back on his arms as though they were levers, hard as they could, hard enough that they heard both shoulders pop. The only sound that came from the man was a murmur of surprise, a grunt, and then his attempts at breathing as his body struggled. They had already broken his nose. Using their weight, they pressed down on the top half of his body as hard as possible, but Prany was already out of breath. There wasn't a lot more strength left in him, he realized.

Years in a cell. The two of them wrestling as quietly as they could to build up stamina.

It wasn't enough. Before panic could set in, the interrogator freed himself from them and collapsed onto the floor. They braced themselves for him to shout, but he didn't. The towel was stuck in his mouth, already soaking up his blood. He crawled slowly toward the door, both of his arms dragging strangely along his sides. Vang grabbed the interrogator's waist, pulled him back across the floor, and together they knelt and pressed their weight on him again.

Because of Prany's hand, Vang was holding the hunting knife. He grabbed the interrogator's hair and pushed his head down and began to stab him in his side above his belt. The interrogator bit down hard on the towel and screamed and his eyes welled and reddened. He flopped like a fish out of water. Prany shoved the towel deeper into the interrogator's mouth and weighed his knee down against him. He watched as Vang kept stabbing him, faster, all across his side, the carpet beginning to grow dark and thick and wet. His glasses fell off, but Vang ignored this, kept stabbing. Then he leaned down and spoke into the interrogator's ear as his body jerked. Prany didn't hear what Vang said. He watched Vang's mouth moving beside the ear and watched as Vang gripped the knife with both hands and pushed down into the back of the throat, the blade slipping down slowly at first and then softly.

And then it was done. The interrogator went still. Vang let go of the knife, which was still in the man. It was like a piece of rock had sprouted from his neck.

Quickly, they took off their towels and shoved them against the interrogator's body to soak up the rest of the blood. They headed into the bathroom, where Vang vomited, kneeling over the toilet. The Fanta and the beer and all the food he had eaten slushed into the toilet bowl. He shut his eyes. He laughed. He laughed louder and Prany covered the doctor's mouth. Prany turned on all the water spouts, the shower head, and the faucet, and he helped Vang up and they began to wash themselves. They opened all the shampoos and unwrapped the soaps and cleaned themselves and each other as fast as possible, as thoroughly as possible, all without looking at the mirror.

They got back into the clothes they had come there with, the clothes that had been given to them. They looked once more at the interrogator on the floor, at his open eyes, the knife in him, his arms crooked. The wet carpet and the towels growing more dark.

They left the inn, the two of them crossing the lobby where there was that faint music, and hurried past the courtyard down the road through the forest. They didn't look back.

Vang handed Prany what little money they had left and said, "You find Auntie. Go."

They had forgotten to clean Vang's glasses. Prany took them off him as they walked down the tree-lined road, trying to rub the blood away as quickly as possible. The scratches on the lenses were dyed red. Prany's breathing became erratic and he began to shiver. And then he stopped on the road and clung to Vang, pressing their foreheads together, wanting to be close to him one last time, to hold the only person he knew anymore one last time.

"Come with me," Prany said. "Please."

Vang, ignoring him, took back his glasses and said, "And then you find Alisak. You find him. Go."

So they parted by the highway, the ferryboat long gone. Prany walked back to the bus station and Vang crossed the road and shouted, once, up into the air, an animallike noise, a bellow, his shape growing fainter as he descended the slope, before his journey home, to swim in the reservoir for the first time in his life.

The bus heading north was a small repurposed military truck that reeked of hay rot, and when it turned into the station lot, he hurried on. The old man who had been waiting on the bench all this time got on as well. They sat across from each other in the dark. They were the only ones.

Prany kept shivering and was out of breath. He tried to sleep, but when he shut his eyes, he saw the strange way the man's arms had dragged across the floor—the towels around him as though pale moss had begun to grow on his body. When the truck sped over a pothole, he thought he was going to vomit, but the nausea went away. He forced himself to stay awake, focusing his gaze on the narrow strip of the receding road that was visible through a gap in the tarp: the borders of fields, a billboard that slipped away, the tail of a large animal, and the sun going down.

He was engulfed by the sound of rushing air and the rattle of the truck bed. There was also the knowledge that one other passenger was on the truck with him. He looked for the old man's silhouette in the shadows across from him but couldn't find him. He wondered if the man had switched seats. Whether his shoulder was now a breath away from his. Who was this old man? What kind of life had he lived for seven years? Prany fought a sudden desire to swing his arm, swing into the dark, and jump. When he thought he finally would, when he couldn't stand it anymore, the truck pulled into the next station, and Prany leaped off, crossed the lot, and switched to another bus.

He was following Auntie's directions. These whispers of narratives from fellow prisoners who would occasionally pass on information to them. It seemed the only thing he could lean on. As the hours passed, as he kept traveling and keeping himself awake, he kept expecting the touch of someone beside him, a voice. Or for the bus to stop, for a car to appear behind them, for a roadblock or a checkpoint. Gunfire. For him to be pulled away.

But all Prany ever encountered was a group of soldiers gathered on the side of the road, wearing the same green uniforms the prison guards wore, ignoring the bus as it drove by. Before the soldiers vanished, he watched through the gap in the tarp as they gathered around a farmer who had his wrists bound and was kneeling in the grass.

It was evening by the time he arrived in Phonsavan. He was the only one to get off the bus. He left the station and walked toward the center of the town, searching for any points of recognition, of a town that had perhaps rebuilt and recovered. But it was desolate, hardly there at all, only what was left of the land. Even the abandoned tanks were gone. There were craters along the side of the road and debris everywhere, more than he remembered: the dismantled structures of what had once been homes, the school, the broken head of a Buddha lying on its side with a single enormous eye staring blankly back at him.

Up ahead, there was one brick building intact. Its yard was littered with plastic jugs. He almost didn't stop until he remembered that it was the town hospital. He walked up to the door that Noi had shot and he stepped in, catching the shapes of people asleep on the floor, sharing a frayed cotton blanket, the moonlight revealing them waking and shielding their faces against him as though he were a weapon.

He left them alone, kept going. He didn't see anyone else. Out in the night now, he began to feel looser, more awake and aware; it was good to walk, to be out of the bus. He picked up a leaf, spun the stem between his fingers. He moved away from his exhaustion and stayed with the fact that at this moment he was experiencing a physical freedom. That he was walking. That he could do so all night if he stayed in the shadows. That there was a sky and it was enormous and unbroken. That it was quiet and clear and that what they had been imagining for so long was now done.

When a wind came, he let the leaf go. Then, approaching the town, he saw to his surprise what had once been the heart of it: the night market, aglow. He stayed on the periphery, under a long, rotting balcony, peering across at the old stalls where he could make out three vendors gathered in a corner, trying to sell their ceramics and baskets, though mostly they were talking to each other, drinking tea, keeping each other company. In one stall, under a hanging lamp, a woman re-folded a textile, and he saw the towels all over the floor again. As though they had given their torturer some courtesy after-ward. He didn't know why they did that.

A man walked by, and Prany, turning, almost bumped into him. Prany froze. The man didn't notice and headed toward a side street. He was pulling off gloves and dressed in a pale uniform Prany had never seen. He thought at first the man must be Pathet Lao, but then Prany caught sight of two actual soldiers: they were checking the papers of the vendors and their goods, one of them pocketing a tiny, ceramic teacup.

Hurrying down toward the river, staying in the shadows, Prany kept looking for somebody, someone else, anyone, faces.

He followed the bank until he reached a large settlement, moving up a slope. A myriad cluster of wooden huts, clay houses, and shanties with metal roofs. Some had collapsed and had never been rebuilt; others had changed over the years. They were dark, though, and it was impossible to tell if anyone actually lived there anymore. Yet after all this, after all the identities and shapes and lifetimes the settlement had gone through on that hill, it had survived.

All night, Prany had been resisting this. But he wanted to see it one last time. To approach this neighborhood again one last time. As though he still lived in this corner of town that had been here as far back in his life as the moon was high above him. As though there remained some part of him somewhere in one of those shanties far up the slope where there was a hot plate and stacks of newspapers they had used for almost everything. Where he would fix an antenna for his father in the morning, all so the man could catch an hour of a radio show. Where a woman trying to siphon electricity off the town wires was electrocuted one morning, and the way they had avoided her body for days, unsure of how long a body could carry a current. Where Prany had once watched Alisak, six years old, swinging a coat hanger at an approaching man in order to protect his mother.

They had all taken care of each other. Where had they all gone? It startled him to be suddenly thinking of parents at all. So many of them on this hill, including theirs, had vanished early on, had died in the war, left, or had become abstractions, erasing themselves so completely in the opium they were hired to harvest and then stole and became addicted to.

He had come here once, during the war, before they had been recruited by the nurses, and hid the one thing he had of his father's up under the eave of what had been their home: a fountain pen. This great luxury of writing. Ink and paper. How the man saved the ink for so long it had, in the last year of his life, dried up. Prany had wondered, when he came, if the pen had survived, knowing it hadn't.

They had nine years together. Before his father died. Two years longer than the years Prany was imprisoned. To him, now, always a lifetime. But it was never long enough to know anything about the man other than he built roads for the country and was often gone. That he liked coffee and the radio. That he had been good to them, though he always preferred being alone. But that one day, because they begged him, he taught the three of them how to drive his motorbike on this river road Prany was standing on now, tonight. The man's shirt pocket always stuffed with cigarettes and a notebook, one Prany never got a chance to see.

His father the secret poet.

Years later, in the chaos of a firefight, Prany watched as a farmer picked up and brought a live grenade to his stomach to shield the blast from the three of them. They had been wandering the mountains in the east and had been running toward an abandoned truck that was blocking the passage.

As the grenade detonated, as the man's shirt ballooned before he sank to his knees, Prany thought of his father—the smell of him, his poor posture, the permanent tar stains on his fingers. How in the early mornings as Noi slept, Prany would sneak out ahead of him, climb a tree, and wait for his father's motorbike to pass under along the road.

How Prany loved this. This private vantage. The hill not yet awake. And how his father always slowed and reached up to grab his son's bare feet before driving on. Their eyes meeting. The touch of his father still there on his heels, like the brush from a feather, as Prany climbed back down.

•

When he turned around, a girl appeared from behind a lamppost and approached him. She was smoking a cigarette and clicked her tongue. Before Prany could speak or flee, the girl slipped her arm under his, and they were leaving the road together, following the river again but heading farther away from the town.

"You Prany?" she said, in a whisper.

"I know five people by that name," Prany said. "Two boys and three girls."

This made her smile. The closeness of her in the dark

startled him. She smelled of the river. Her breath was sour. He felt the movement of her arm against his pocket and he stopped, gripped her wrist, and found some of his money in her grasp. She stayed where she was, close to him, smoking her cigarette and staring at him until he backed away.

"Where's Auntie?" he said.

"Ask her," she said, and pointed at an open shed up ahead.

It was an old fishermen's shed with a thatched roof. As he approached, he noticed a younger girl, around thirteen, sitting on the wooden counter in the back that had been used to clean fish. She was wearing a pair of men's trousers, the cuffs rolled up, the waist cinched with a thick rope.

"Careful where you step," the younger girl said as he ducked under the roof.

For a moment, he thought she was talking about a bomb. But she was simply looking down at a path of moonlight on the ground. So Prany joined her on the counter and looked down, unsure of what she was focusing on until he spotted a caterpillar slowly making its way along its border.

"If you wait long enough, it'll go into the light," she said, and swung her legs in the air.

"Long time to wait," Prany said.

She shrugged, held the edge of the counter, and stared at him. They didn't know each other. In the sudden stillness in the shed, he began to feel his own exhaustion again. It was like his own skeleton was trembling inside of him. His hunger returned, also, but the thought of food nauseated him. He took out another bill and asked where Auntie was.

When she didn't respond, he asked what her name was.

"What's yours?"

"Me? I'm a vampire."

"That's not funny," the girl said. "What happened to your hand?"

"What happened to your face?" Prany said.

There was a thick shrapnel scar running across the girl's cheek.

"Bah," she said. "The boys think it's pretty. It's pretty, no?" She angled her face at him as though she were posing for a camera. She was whispering, too.

"Khit," she said. "My name. Khit."

He did not yet recognize the name.

The other girl, who had been standing guard outside the shed, clicked her tongue. The two soldiers he had seen in the square earlier walked down the street. Before he was aware of his own body stiffening, he felt Khit's growing smaller as she folded herself behind him like a cat.

"Someone looking for you?" he said, sliding her behind him on the counter.

"Touch me again and I'll kill you," she said.

Together, they watched the other girl approach the soldiers. The soldiers whistled. The girl laughed at something they said and took one of their hats and slipped it on, angling her hip. Then she waved the money she had taken from Prany, slipped her arms around them both, and led them away. She didn't look back.

When the footsteps faded, Prany said, "What will happen to her?"

"Her? You mean, what will happen to them," Khit said, and giggled as she crawled out from behind him.

"Please," Prany said. "Where's Auntie?"

Khit continued to ignore him, searching for the caterpillar on the floor.

"It's there," Prany said, pointing.

She leaned forward to look. "You have food?" she said.

He stood and went over to a bin in the corner and rooted around, but she said she already checked. He took out his last bill from the envelope. She said it really wasn't much use here when there was hardly any food, but she took the money anyway, tucking it into her sock.

As he sat back down, he noticed some blood on his fingernails, on his shirt, too, and wondered if she had noticed. She was pushing her thumb along the old knife marks on the counter.

He caught a metallic taste in his mouth and spat, and then he held himself, pacing the hut a little. He wanted this girl to keep talking.

"The cars," Prany said. "I haven't seen a single car."

"Thailand," Khit said. "Or in storage. Gas prices. No money. Gone."

He asked how long the town had been like this, the country. He thought of him and Vang getting out at the bus station earlier today. Was it only today?

Khit replied it always was. That it had always been like this. "Where have you been? People died or didn't come back. Mostly only the soldiers now, here. Those two. Always those two. They choose a house where there is someone trying to live or spend the night, go in, take whatever they want, sell it or trade it with the truck that comes every week with their cigarettes and their bottles. Sometimes, some travelers pass through, but not many. Last year, I saw a North Korean. You ever seen a North Korean? Or a Russian? Different uniforms. Smell different, too. The North Korean gave me a cigarette. He spoke some French. Not bad."

Prany mentioned the uniformed man he had seen earlier, the one he had almost bumped into. He asked what kind of uniform that was.

"Not police," Khit said, eyeing the road. "They clear fields. Bomb detectors. Like I said, where have you been? All these questions. They're everywhere. The only good work you can find. You'll see signs. Shows you where you can go and where you can't. Just like me. I'm your sign today." She pointed out toward the distance. "You should go to the hospital."

"The hospital?"

"I mean, the old one. The old house."

"The farmhouse?"

"The hospital, the farmhouse. You're making my head spin." Khit pulled out a new envelope from her waistband. "You're supposed to go meet Auntie there. First you go around back to the river. You meet the boat. And then you go to the farmhouse and wait for Auntie to come. And then you give her this."

"The farmhouse," Prany said, and opened the envelope that was filled with more money, American dollars this time.

"I don't know why she goes there," Khit said. "No one else does. Too scary for me. It's just her and those ghosts."

He thought the girl meant the history there.

"That's a lot of dollars," she said.

"Who gave this to you?"

"People who know Auntie," Khit said.

"Did you take any of it?"

"You stupid enough to cross Auntie?" she said. "Who are you? That's enough for two people to get out, no?"

"I don't think so," he said, and waved the envelope at her.

When Prany stood, she tugged on his sleeve and said, "You play cards? We can play together if you want. I know someone with some cards. The soldiers won't come back for hours."

"You know their route," he said.

"Everyone knows their route," she said.

He stepped over the caterpillar and crossed the hut, trying to remember the last time he had talked to someone a lot younger than he was. The last time he had been inside a fisherman's hut. From the entrance, he could make out the top of the hill settlement, dark. Briefly, he remembered that garden, the handful of soil, that child. The caterpillar kept moving along the edge of the light.

"Where will you end up?" Khit said.

He didn't know. Thailand or France, he thought, recalling how they, the three of them, had always said this.

"France," Khit said. "I would like to go to France."

He tried to feel something about his leaving, but there was nothing. It was as though it had already happened, that a long time had already passed from this point here. From outside came the faint sound of a boat. Water lapping. Prany didn't turn, knew the girl was watching him. He said, "Got to go," and headed down to the river where the boat woman was waiting for him.

So she had survived. He couldn't tell if she recognized him. How many children had she provided passage for up and down this river? Did she continue to? He fought the urge to run to her when he saw her. But she didn't speak or even look at him as he slipped quietly in, and then she steered him downriver, the water holding the reflection of the night. The moon in the wake. He dipped his fingers into the river. River of his childhood.

The woman steered with the crux of her elbow. They motored past a line of dead trees. The shapes of men in uniforms, too far away to hear them. He thought of his father again. The pen. He searched for the monk's house, but couldn't recall where it was. He wondered where all the monks had gone, whether the temple was there high above the river, invisible now in the dark. How many times had they paused, walking, and looked up at its corridors aglow with distant firelight?

He thought of how, when they were hiding in the mountains before they were caught, someone would stack pebbles on the ground, one on top of the other, every day in front of their shelter. These small towers in shades of earth that grew in number and never fell. And that, when they were finished, no one ever touched. As though in their completion the person had created something else.

Where was Vang right now? Back to the place he called

home. Uncertain of the days Vang had left before he was inevitably found, arrested, and tried. Knowing all this, even as Prany kept urging him to leave with him, Vang hadn't wanted to go anywhere else. *I want to find my rooftop*, he kept saying, Prany never knowing what that meant. In their last year, he had given up persuading the doctor not to part with him, but he would forever be unsure if it was to honor his friend's wish or because they had both been so broken he couldn't push it any further anymore.

They traveled for almost an hour. Then, after a bend, the woman slowed the boat, approaching a bank, running parallel with it, and it was then that she leaned over and gently placed a hand on his shoulder, squeezing once. And as a space opened up between the trees, Prany leaped off without her ever stopping, without him looking back.

He was out in the open. He listened to the fading engine for as long as possible as he made his way across the hills. Signs with large symbols began to appear on wooden posts indicating where bombs had been cleared and where they hadn't been. He followed the clearance signs, stopping at a row of stone jars to peer inside them. He passed a log with a pair of weathered slippers on them. He felt the moonlight on his shoulders and he didn't know why he kept thinking of those towels more than anything else.

What Prany knew was that in a short while the farm would be visible. And it was. The fields came up from the distance and then what was left of that house that had been a secret hospital, where they had nursed the wounded, driven supplies, mopped the blood off the floors, learned how to set a broken leg, suture, administer an IV, how to fire a rifle and a pistol. All this for some money and a place to live more than a decade ago. The doctors and the nurses paying them double if they were crazy enough to retrieve medicine from another hospital in the valley, racing the bombers.

What did it matter anymore?

The truth he knew tonight was that the vehicle that pulled up to recruit them could have been from the other side and they wouldn't have cared if it meant, on that day, the promise of shelter and food. Because they were children who had nowhere else to go. And because, for what seemed like the first time, the people who had approached them had been kind.

He was suddenly tired again. It swept over him as he hurried past more signs, startling a rat who scurried on ahead of him. Prany crossed the first tobacco field, his eyes never leaving the house that now had half of its roof missing and most of the glass windows blown out. Smaller, more compact than he remembered, but looming all the same like the beacon that it had been when they used to race back with supplies in the dark, clinging to the tug of that one candle in the upstairs window in the backdrop of that flattened night landscape.

The courtyard had turned wild. And the fountain at the center was full of, mysteriously, soil. Rather than try the door, he hauled himself up through a window frame and slid in, reaching down to the dusty wooden floor. Always preferring an indirect way, as Alisak would have said. When Prany stood, he saw he had left a handprint in the dust. Like a single wide leaf.

He was in what had been a dining room and where they had placed more of the wounded when the ward was full. It was also where he had spied two doctors embracing each other one night, against a corner, the sudden need for that intimacy that could have had everything or nothing to do with attraction. How he could feel the urgency of that embrace from across the room where he had paused by the curtains, a bucket hanging from his wrist.

Always to his surprise, it was this house his mind had often leaped to these past years. Not the town, but here. The way he roamed the halls. Entered the rooms and opened drawers as though each held a mysterious treasure. The way they were all together. Wanting this place as though it were something he could endlessly carry with him.

He knew where he was. He knew every corner, every panel

of flooring that sang and moaned. There were even a few paintings on the walls. It almost made him smile. So they didn't take
all of them. Still lifes of fruit. Ships in a port. A portrait of a
girl that used to make him blush, her eyes always following
him. Some of the arms of the high chandelier had broken off, as
though someone had tried to swing from it.

Prany entered a room where there were more beds and a
doctor's coat hanging on a hook. He swung the coat on, the
dust rising from its shoulders and floating in the moonlight.
In a pocket, he found a folded piece of paper that he brought
to a window. Someone had drawn a circle on it, in a decade-
old pencil. Just that. He put it back into the pocket as though
knowing it belonged only there, in a private memory.

He crossed into the foyer and climbed the wide stairs that
were covered by a carpet that had thinned so much the threads
tore with each of his steps. On the landing lay the carcass of a
rabbit, shriveled to just its dark, mangy fur. The air coming in
everywhere, thick with dust.

It could have been the middle of the night or closer to
dawn. Prany had lost track of time. He didn't know how
much of it he himself had either. By now, someone would have
long discovered the interrogator in the room. That young man
or even the daughter, perhaps, her child.

This morning, he had woken with Vang in a cell narrow

enough so that they could extend their arms and touch both walls that were stained and darkened by years of them doing this. This afternoon, they had pinned an old man down on a floor and they had done what they did, together. Every morning, he heard the shriek of a baton on cell doors and stood in his exhaustion and the hurt of his body. There was always the hurt. The recovery and the starting over again.

Now his body was heavy as sand, but he sensed a new focus as he walked down the wallpapered hall to the last room, where the door was ajar. He was beyond tired, to a point that seemed like clarity. He heard a noise downstairs, thought it must be the rat, and then he entered the room in the corner where they had often spent the hours.

An empty chair was pulled up toward the window. Outside, there was a view of his entire route through the valley. The bright night and the air coming in. As Prany crossed the room, stepping over a hole in the floor, he was already reaching for the piano, dust-covered, against the wall.

He lay awake, curled beside the hole in the floor. His body a dead thing for hours until the sun entered through the window and over him. He couldn't remember if a day or two had passed. He had been trying to find a way into sleep. When he lifted himself up, his disorientation magnified, unmoored by the largeness of the room, the walls far away. For a moment, he forgot everything. It was almost like peace. And then he slid against a corner near the window and rocked back and forth until the shivering in his body went away.

His throat was on fire. His bones like ice. He doubled over and gagged, though nothing came out. His stomach hollow and raw as though someone had scraped it with a knife.

When he turned toward the morning, seeking the sun, Prany spotted a figure emerging from one of the stone jars in the distance: first an arm, then another, then a head—someone who had, perhaps, found something inside of the jar and was crossing the tobacco field. Only now in the light did Prany notice that some of the sticks they had staked into the ground had survived.

The figure ran across the field into the courtyard. Closer,

he recognized that it was Khit. She avoided the front entrance as well, using the window, and from the corner of this second-floor room, he listened to her enter the way he had, the house giving in to her. He could picture clearly the rooms she was entering by the sound of her footsteps in relation to where he was, something they often did with Vang or with the nurses, always aware of where everyone was, always needing to be aware.

It took her some time to enter the piano room. When she did, she didn't notice him. She stood in front of the instrument, opened the cover, and pressed down on a key. Then another. The notes, out of tune, lasted, filling the space.

"Play something for me," Prany said.

She jumped. She jumped, he noticed, but didn't turn. Then she did, slowly, considering him there shivering in that corner before playing some more notes.

He asked what she was doing here. Why she had followed him. Khit didn't answer him immediately. She kept playing.

And then she said, "I don't know how to save the money. To pay Auntie. To get out."

"Where do you live?" Prany said.

"All over."

"Not on the hill? The settlement? Where are your parents?"

"Mr. Vampire," she said. "You okay? Is it your hand?"

She looked back at him in that corner.

148

"You ask too many questions," Prany said.

"You've been asking the questions," Khit said.

"You Thai? Hmong?"

"A little bit of everything."

Then he asked again whether anyone was looking for her.

She shrugged. Her hands hovered over the piano keys. "What does it matter? I'm small and quick."

"That's you."

"Yeah. And smart."

"You survived because you're small and quick and smart."

"Last time I checked," Khit said, and raised a fist in the air, approaching him. She stopped at the perimeter of the hole in the floor and sat down, slipping her legs into the space so that they vanished. "I like that coat," she said.

"What did you find in the jar?" he said.

With her legs in the hole, she lay back and stared up at the ceiling. "My mother was brought here. She'd been injured. I was with my father; we couldn't get to her. But I used to come here on occasion, after. I used to look for things that might belong to her, but I don't do that anymore. It's a strange house and I don't like being here."

"Then go."

She stayed where she was, lying down. "Do you have food now?"

"Try the kitchen," Prany said.

"I don't like going down there." She pointed into the hole but kept looking up at the broken ceiling. "Are you a bad man?"

"No," he said. "I don't know. Maybe. Yes. Yes, I think I am."

"I don't think you are."

"I think you should go."

"Take me with you," Khit said.

He remembered her. Just then, now. It was like she had surfaced from water and he had been there the whole time, waiting. He remembered her mother. The name. The ward. He remembered it all.

"Who are you?" Khit said. "Where have you been? What have you done?"

He wasn't shaking anymore. He wiped his face and stood from the corner and walked past her to the piano. He knelt and popped open a panel on the bottom of it and reached up inside. She watched from the floor, upside down, as his fingers searched the inside of the piano for all the things they used to hide in there.

They stole from the dead. They took a ring or cut a piece of a shirtsleeve using a scalpel or collected a woman's prayer beads and put these all into pouches and hid them, not really knowing why and not telling anyone—some compulsion the three of them were guilty of, inexplicably and secretly, with no further intention of doing anything to those objects other than to collect them, to hide them, and to keep them safe.

"You think I'll get out?" Khit said. "One day?"

"You'll get out. Now come help."

He pulled out one pouch after another and they spent the morning opening them, sifting through all the things spread out on the floor for anything they wanted.

•

He waited a full day until it was night again. The girl slept the whole time, curled up by the hole in the floor. He had been drifting in and out, watching her. In what felt like the first time in years, Prany had briefly dreamed of Noi. She had come up on a motorbike and in one uninterrupted motion she had scooped him up, and before he understood what was happening, he was sitting behind her, leaning into her back, the two of them driving away.

He woke thinking of the curve of her arm that felt, when they were younger, like the greatest net. The suddenness of her care. Noi, who always entered his day like a door swinging open.

He heard a noise downstairs. Prany got up and stepped out quietly, softening the creak of the floorboards as much as possible as he followed where he thought the rat must have gone. The hallway continued past the main set of stairs, where there were other rooms with their doors closed. He ignored the rooms and headed straight toward the end of the hall, where there was another set of stairs, this one narrow and enclosed, and he went down in the complete dark before he arrived in the kitchen.

In a wide crack in the floor, a fledgling tree was growing at the entrance. He moved around it, careful not to disturb the leaves. There was still an assortment of pots hanging from the ceiling, the night reflecting off them. Dried herbs a decade old were in a sealed jar. Animals had gotten into a grain sack, which was slumped in a corner with a hole near the base the size of his fist. In the far corner, near a bureau, stood a grand-father clock. If it was working, it was half past three in the morning.

He tried the faucet, heard it exhale. Then he went to a cupboard and collected what was left of the crackers and a can with its label missing. He searched for a can opener, pulling out the empty drawers, the room filling with the sound of the creaking wood.

The rat appeared, following the counter, and vanished under a faded tapestry hanging from the ceiling. The fabric fluttered like a sail, catching a draft. Leaving the can on the counter, Prany approached, pushed the fabric aside where there was the door, a thin horizon of light glowing at the bottom.

Prany was about to go in, but hesitated. He felt the draft on his ankles. Stared down at the light. He leaned against the door. Then he left the kitchen, headed to the wing where they used to keep the bikes, and stepped outside. He didn't stop. He walked away from the house, skirting the field he had come in from, waiting for some sound or movement to break the horizon. Something to enter the valley.

It had all become this, he thought. All this time, it had never occurred to him that if he lived long enough to reenter the world, this new country, it would be empty.

He was still wearing the doctor's coat. Its hem brushed against his calves as he stepped forward past a warning sign into a farther field that had yet to be cleared. When he shut his eyes, Prany saw the towels again, but it didn't affect him as they had before. He clutched his ruined hand and breathed as he took another step. And then another, passing more warning signs.

He kept his eyes shut and walked deeper into the unknown field, following an imaginary line, knowing that something might happen. He listened and waited for it. Heard his pounding heart. The swaying of the doctor's coat and then a distant animal. He kept walking across and waited, waited for the years to slip out of him, and this thought, like a hook caught inside of him, that his life had been formed by departures. Other people's. His own. How it was impossible for him now to define a home. To carry some sense of it. To feel some center to his day.

Prany opened his eyes. He had reached the edge and turned. All this quiet. The clear night. The pale coat on him. The house in the distance, and the ward, and the window behind which, he presumed, the girl was asleep.

He breathed. Again, he listened. He held the folded piece of paper in the coat pocket as he crossed the field once more, back.

•

Someone tall was waiting for him outside the house.

"You're all grown up," she said to Prany as he approached.

She stepped into the moonlight and greeted him. For a year, until they were caught, he and Vang had lived with her in the mountains on the Thai border.

"It's actually a bit cold, isn't it," she said. "But I like that feeling. I want it to last a little longer before the day starts. I like shivering. That sounds silly. But I look forward to it. You must be tired."

She reached for him and he flinched. She ignored this and kept talking. "This morning, I remembered how you learned to weave baskets. When you and Vang were hiding in the mountains with me. You would sneak them down to another village and try to sell them. Bring back food. Most were too scared to, but not you. We were still living seeking cover from an air war that thought so little of us, all of us, weren't we? Our allies. What did the American president say? If you save one country in the middle of this nightmare, then maybe you stop the dominoes from tumbling against each other . . . What is a fucking domino? A Cold War? So many didn't even know the difference between a Communist and an anti-Communist, they just wanted to survive.

"I've missed you, Prany. We're strangers to each other now, yes? Well, I'm here. This has been my life. I send people away. I give them new lives. But I can still think of you much younger, submerging yourself into the river to collect pebbles or watching me behead a chicken on a tree stump. I can think of your laughter and your crying and the smell of you, but it isn't you, is it? That is another life. Four years. It took me four years to find you and then another year to plan how to get word to you, and then two to plan all this, and seven altogether, as you know, for you to come back here. And in that time, I thought of you and Vang every day because I never said

good-bye to you both. Because I escaped. Because I was lucky.
And so tell me: Who am I to you? Who is it that you think of
every day? What do you imagine your life will be like when I
take you across? What were the days like there in the prison
for seven years? Whom did you think of? Am I less of a person
for fleeing when our camp was overrun? For refusing now
to ask how Vang is? Did he ever talk about me? Does he look
as unrecognizable as you are now? Is the person I remember
still inside him? . . . I refuse, I refuse . . . Tell me: Was it worth
what you just did? Was that for you or for Vang, whom you
could not protect in there? Was it for your sister?"

Prany had been by the water fountain that was filled with
dirt. Now he rushed toward her, entering the moonlight, and
reached for her neck. He began to squeeze and she let him.
She hung her arms down and stood there, facing him.

"Was it you?" Prany said, squeezing harder.

A wind came and blew across the valley. He watched her
eyes well and he asked again if it was her who gave them all
up. He felt her go weightless, and he let go. He faced the valley, listening to Auntie collapse and cough. She rubbed her
neck. She spat and wiped her eyes.

Prany took out the envelope with the money and dropped
it beside her.

"There is a young girl," he said. "Upstairs. Take her."

Auntie got up. She pocketed the envelope, rubbed her neck again, and looked over his shoulder. Prany turned to see Khit standing by the open front door, suddenly shy. He wondered how long she had been standing there.

"What does that girl mean to you?" Auntie said. "One of thousands who want to go across."

"I'm staying," Prany said.

"For what?"

"I'll stay and help."

"You'll be caught. You'll be caught for what you just did."

"Then I'll help until I'm caught."

"Then you're a fool."

Prany couldn't tell if she meant what she had just said. He walked back toward Khit and leaned down. He said to her that it was time to go. That if she wanted to, it was time to go now. And he told her he remembered her mother and remembered the good day her mother had selling seven baskets at the market. That she got along with the potter and loved the smell of the night like the one now. Deep grass. That her mother was never afraid.

And then Prany said Alisak's name. He made Khit promise that she would remember that name. That wherever she went, she would remember that name. That she should always ask about that name.

"Promise," he said, and Khit, who had begun to tremble, unable to meet his eyes, did.

And to Auntie he said, "Look for me when you come back across."

And then he took off the doctor's coat. He put it on Khit. It was too long, the hem covering the ground, but she didn't take it off as she hurried across the courtyard.

"Was there a message for me?" Auntie said to Prany. She meant a message from Vang.

He shook his head. With Khit beside her now, Auntie walked over to the fountain and said, "No, Prany. I didn't give you up." She sank her hand into the dirt, came up, and wiped her fingers against her trousers. Then she looked down, regarding Khit.

"Auntie," Prany said. "Do you still have your knife?"

She took out her knife and tossed it to him. Then she tossed him a canteen filled with water. Prany went back inside as the two of them walked across the tobacco field, following the sticks. He picked up the can he had left on the counter. The knife had a can opener attached to it, and he used it, pausing once, his good hand sore. The can had beans inside. It made him laugh a little. They were inedible, dry and sour, but he ate them anyway.

He was no longer shivering. He felt stronger. He felt the

emptiness of this house that had survived and thought about the Tobacco Captain somewhere, perhaps alive. He drank the water Auntie had given him and scanned the broken ceiling that was filled with moonlight. He heard the coo of a bird and the wind.

He had forgotten he could weave a basket.

Prany approached the tapestry once more, pushed it aside, and slid open the door. He went in the way he used to, consumed again by the stale, dusty air that made him cough. He looked straight ahead, ignoring the hall of six mirrors that caught his emaciated, hollow reflection, and entered the ward.

Inside, there were four rows of metal bed frames. Some of them were empty, others had mattresses, and there was one in the middle with a white sheet draped over it like a tablecloth. A metal tray lay flipped over on the floor. Scattered about the tray was a cup, a pair of scissors, and a ball of suturing thread.

The air came in through the broken windows. Everywhere there was moonlight.

From another room, the grandfather clock tolled. And as Prany counted the beats, a shape sat up from the bed with the sheet over it. The man—it was a man—swung his legs over the edge of the bed, his back to Prany. He had gray hair and he was wearing a hospital gown. He slipped his feet into a pair of slippers and walked to the center of the room, where he proceeded to pick up the scissors, the cup, and the sutures, and place them on the tray, which he returned to a table on the far wall. Then he picked up a broom and began to sweep. He moved down the aisle between the beds, past the first one, where Vang used to perform minor surgeries, and headed toward Prany. Prany heard the broom slide across the floor. Footsteps. A strand of the man's hair fell from his forehead and the broom swept it away.

Before he reached Prany, the man stopped.

"Am I done?" he said, looking over Prany's shoulder at the hall of mirrors.

In whatever world he existed in, someone answered, so the man returned the broom to the wall and lay back down on the bed.

It was silent again. Out the window, there was a view of the courtyard, the tangled vines and grass. One day, all of this would be gone. It would be another farm. A room for something else. Prany wondered in what form this man he had just witnessed would exist. If the man would exist at all.

Prany stepped farther in. He passed the bed with the sheet over it, then passed the one where Khit's mother had been. Through the tall windows he spotted the shapes of Auntie and Khit. They were now far, faint in the valley, but he could make out the paleness of the doctor's coat. Something in Auntie's hair, like a firefly, caught the night. It occurred to him the girl never told him what she had found in the stone jar, if she had in fact found something.

A droplet fell on his wrist. He thought it had begun to rain, that he was standing in the far corner where there was the gap in the ceiling. But it was his nose. It was bleeding again. He let it drip, staying by the window frame until he couldn't see Auntie and the girl anymore.

For a little while longer, Prany kept watch. He tapped the wall and reached into his shirt pocket, remembering that the piece of paper with a circle drawn on it was not there but in the doctor's coat. And then Prany walked across the ward, slipped into the last bed in the last row, and slept.

NOI

(1969)

Some nights after she finished her duties in the ward, she would slip out and wander the farmhouse the way she once had, years before. She walked through what had been the great rooms and the corridors, through all the moonlight, stepping over a nurse asleep on the floor or lying against a beam that had fallen but was too heavy to move.

All that time unaware that she was spinning the ring on her thumb until she happened to look down or felt the cold of it suddenly, as though it had just appeared like some gift from a ghost who was accompanying her.

It was, in fact, a gift from the Frenchman who owned this house, though she never told anyone that, not her brother or Alisak. They figured she had found it or poached it from somebody, and she didn't correct them.

At first, she kept it because it was probably worth something. But that changed over time. She thought of how they had once crossed a rice field only to return a week later to that same field gone, one corner of it turned into a mass grave someone had stopped covering, as though they had changed their minds halfway through, the shovel sticking up from a hill of dirt. So they had finished it themselves, as quickly as possible, taking turns while the others kept an eye on the road, all of them avoiding looking down.

How they never spoke about these things, but kept going, day after day, for as long as they could.

And for Noi, this growing need, the more they witnessed and came upon, to keep some part of herself from a long time ago. Some record of it. This one thing. And the private, inexplicable fear that if she were to lose it, she wouldn't be anyone anymore.

Noi, whose recurring dream at the farmhouse was that as she passed that hall of mirrors, hurrying to find somebody, something—what was it?—she wasn't there in the reflection.

She wondered, too, what proof of herself, of them, would remain in this house after they were gone. The motorcycles, perhaps. The piano with its loose panel and those pouches and their fingerprints on each and every key they touched but never pressed down. There was the dirt stain from her shirt against a closet wall as she and her brother sought cover from a bomb. The mop she used in the ward without realizing how bloody the water was until she saw it all over her palms. So she had pulled up the hem of her shirt to clean herself as she kept walking through the house, awake—she could never sleep here—recalling what it looked like back then, which falling wallpaper or piece of broken furniture had outlived those years.

She was still surprised she had found herself at this house again after so long. The three of them had jumped into a jeep for the first time, trusting two strangers, and as they sped toward the Plain of Jars, her brother and Alisak leaning out and luxuriating in the cool rush of wind—when was the last time they had been in a vehicle together?—Noi suddenly knew where they were going.

She had been walking with Alisak when a car appeared on the river road one afternoon, slowed, and a man, leaning across, rolled down the passenger-side window. Two girls a few years older than Noi were seated in the back. She was twelve, Alisak a year older. In six months, the town would be taken over and they would begin wandering the country.

They had never seen the driver before, this foreigner, didn't know who he was then. They had never seen the girls either. The man spoke in a mix of French and some Lao words he had learned. He said he needed help for a party and revealed the money. It was more than they had ever seen. He said it was only a night's work. That he was in a hurry and if they didn't want the job he would go on.

Alisak shrugged, reached for the door, but the man held up his hand.

"Just her," he said.

Noi looked at the girls and at the money. The girls waved for her to join them. So she told Alisak she would see him later and got in, the two others in the back sliding over for her. Then they drove past Alisak, who was tossing a stick on the side of the road, their eyes meeting briefly, and then they were heading across the valley and the tobacco fields to the house.

At the house, she was given a uniform—the fabric so clean and crisp it made her shiver—and for the rest of the evening she moved back and forth from the kitchen to all the rooms, refilling a silver tray with food and glasses of wine.

It wasn't odd to her that there was hardly anyone there because she had never been to a party like this. Or perhaps it was that the house was so large, the rooms felt empty. What she realized was that he—the man who had been driving—was the only Frenchman. And that no one noticed her. She recognized a local policeman. He was speaking about a thief whose identity the group around him was guessing.

I think it is that mean-spirited restaurant owner. No, it is most certainly a fisherman.

In another room, she heard a man talking about food shortages. The changing temperature of the river.

The hours passed, Noi catching moments of conversations

and, coming from somewhere she never found, distant music. Then the party was done and she was told to help clean up, putting away the food, washing and drying the dishes, which she stacked inside the kitchen cabinets using a stepladder, promising herself she would not trip and fall.

When she was finally excused, she stepped out into a hall to a vast silence. Some of the lights still on, but dim. She had no idea what time it was. She was exhausted and hungry, but there was also the understanding that there was enough money in the back pocket of her pants to last months. And that she was still in these fresh, new clothes.

Standing by the entrance, alone, she realized she was supposed to walk back to town. And she almost did walk out, but instead she turned and crossed over to the other wing of the house, following a long corridor with paintings and a row of small chandeliers. She had walked down here a few times in the evening—it was those small chandeliers she had noticed, the way the light fell, it seemed, in a multitude of directions—and even in her tiredness, she luxuriated in the strange light, knowing that she might never walk down a corridor like this again.

She walked wondering if she could come back. And what she would tell Prany and Alisak when she returned to them. She reminded herself to tell them about the changing river temperature. Then she wondered if they were there by the river or with the boat woman or somewhere else, somewhere new, like her.

She was thinking of the way she had caught Alisak's eyes outside the car window, the two of them looking at each other the way they had begun to, silently and often, as though each of them wanted to tell the other something but didn't know how—she was thinking of that moment when the car had sped away from him when she entered the enormity of the dining room with its long table, its paintings and high-back chairs.

She was ignoring her exhaustion, her eyes wanting to con-sume everything, but slow to find, in the back corner, the two girls she had come in with. They were lying on the floor, asleep, without their clothes, curled up like two animals by the feet of the Frenchman, who was in a corner chair, wearing a loose robe that revealed his own nakedness. It appeared he was also asleep.

She stayed quiet, startled, as the Frenchman opened his bloodshot eyes, sensing her presence there by the long table, and then focusing on her. He smiled. Then he stood—he was tall and extremely thin and pale, she could see the ridges of his rib cage—and he dragged the chair over to her. He motioned for her to take a seat by the table and Noi, terrified, did what she was told. Then he brought his own chair close enough so that, facing her, their knees almost touched. He leaned forward a little, staring at her, and she could smell the deep stink of his breath, the smell in between his legs. She could hear his heavy breathing as he leaned back and tightened his robe, covering himself, and placed his hands behind his head. There was a sudden clarity to him that surprised her.

And when he spoke, it was like in the car, the man using a mix of French and Lao again: "Did you know? In France. There used to be parties where everyone wore masks. Centuries ago. It was supposed to bring people of different classes and histories together. The anonymity and equality of it. A countess could dance with someone, say, of the middle class and neither would be the wiser. It was also, of course, an invitation for recklessness and criminality. What do you think? What if I had masks at my parties? Would it be equality or criminality?"

She didn't understand all of what he was saying. The man sighed.

"I wish I had a mask," he said. "Find one for me, will you? Maybe there is a place in your town. Maybe someone could make me one. Do you know a mask maker? I want the border of it speckled in jewels. I want the nose to be very long."

In the dim light of the room, he showed her his profile and mimicked extending his nose with his hand.

"They say I should have fled a long time ago," he said. "Fled with all of my fellow countrymen. That I'm foolish to still be here while your country implodes. Foolish to throw my parties. And that perhaps I am a maniac for violence. What do you think? Is it foolish or maniacal of me? Do you understand these words in French? I do not know them in your language, but I did in German. I don't remember anymore. I used to know German words. I would kneel beside a dying Nazi, just a boy, and promise to save his life if he taught me some words. They always taught me some words. All that yearning for one moment longer in life. That brief recognition of a world beyond one field or bombed-out town where they lay dying. That there might be a future beyond there. What hope. Tell me, do you still have parents?"

He stopped, as though he had heard a noise. There was no noise. She was holding her breath, and then breathing when she couldn't hold it any longer. Repeating this. She was thinking of a German boy—she had understood that part of what he said—and then the way he had phrased the last question. And then for what seemed like the first time in a long time she thought of them, her parents, or just her father, clinging to a fading image of him, young, not entirely sure anymore if it was true or from her imagination.

The Frenchman brought his hand down and reached across to rub the collar of her shirt.

"You stained it," he said, but she didn't look. "You can take off the clothes now and give them to me or I can take my money back. Do you understand?"

Noi had been focusing on the two girls on the floor still asleep. She didn't speak. She did nothing. Then she heard a clock chime in a far room, and the man reached behind her and took his money. Slipping it into a pocket in his robe, he leaned back again, studying her once more, and then stuck one of his fingers into his mouth, wetting it. He slid off a ring he was wearing, reached across and slipped it over her thumb, and thanked her for her services.

She made to leave, quickly, but he was the one who left. He returned his chair to where it had been, swinging it over the two girls who were still asleep, and then he opened a side door that was a part of the wall, and vanished.

Not long after, she would return to the front entrance and walk out of this house, returning to the town at dawn to find her brother with a hat over his face, asleep against a fisherman's hut across from the hill community where they had all been born but knew hardly anyone there anymore. She would search for Alisak.

But before all this, before that walk, before the days that went on, and before she moved further away from the memory of that man and this house, she went to the girls in the corner of the room. She sat on the chair that was warm from the heat of that man, and leaned down to check each of their pulses.

•

Even now, years later, Noi could still feel the warmth of them as she found herself entering this room on what would be the last evening at the farmhouse. Again, she sat down in that corner chair that had survived, the cushion frayed and faded from the weather. She imagined the shapes of those two girls curled up on the floor. Imagined them standing and leaving, too.

She heard footsteps. When Vang appeared, he didn't notice her at first. Thinking he was alone, Vang approached a window that was still intact and looked out at the fields where he had stumbled out three days earlier, out of his mind. In the moonlight, the doctor was just a shadow. Noi heard him tapping his fingers against his chest—something, she had noticed, he had recently begun to do. She stood, the creak of the chair causing him to turn, and she walked around the long table and met him there, by that window.

"We leave tonight," Vang said.

"I should wake Alisak."

"No. Let him sleep a little longer. He'll need the rest. The helicopters won't be here for a while."

She nodded, even though he wasn't looking at her. "Were you looking for me?"

"Yes," the doctor said.

"Is Prany all right?"

"Yes. Yes, of course. He's on his shift. No. I'm sorry. I didn't mean that. There's a woman in the ward. First row. She was asking for you."

Noi spun the ring around her thumb. Outside, beyond the fountain, the sticks Alisak had planted in the fields swayed slightly from the wind.

"Will she be coming with us? That woman."

The doctor shook his head. Noi had known the answer for a while now. She wasn't sure why she asked. And then Vang looked at her and said she had saved his life and he had never thanked her for it.

"Yes." Noi smiled. "You already did. That day."

Vang didn't respond, but tapped his chest some more. She moved closer to the window and wiped her breath away. She caught a faint blinking light on the horizon. Then it went away. She thought of Alisak again. She wanted to say to the doctor just then that even in the madness, he had given the three of them time and a place to be together, but she wasn't sure if he would understand, or if it was even a thought she wanted to say out loud.

She thought about whom she would be able to find if they were all wearing masks.

"Tonight," Vang said again, and began walking away.

"Thailand or France?" Noi called to him, her voice echoing in the long room.

From the corridor, under the one chandelier that remained hanging from the ceiling, Vang turned.

"France."

•

Where was that man now? She never discovered an answer to this, never knew if he had eventually escaped or had stayed to confront this world becoming, minute by minute, unrecognizable. Whether he was, in fact, a fool or a maniac.

Sometimes, over the years, the Tobacco Captain would visit her in a dream, always in the guise of someone else: a farmer who once provided her shelter; or a soldier she had stumbled on one morning, running by her in the valley without acknowledging her presence; or often, later, a doctor wearing a pale coat as he appeared around the bend of a wooded path and asked if she wanted to take a walk with him.

And always she did walk with him, certain of their destination, but never remembering when she woke. Never understanding why she kept him company at all, only that in dreams he was kind and, almost like a young boy, shy.

It was Alisak whom she walked with that day. Eventually, she found him on the river road, in his arms a crate of food he had found. His mouth already full as she accompanied him to that old tree across the hill and for the first time stopped to embrace him, wanting, more than anything, to feel him around her, by her. To feel every year they had been in each other's life.

He dropped the crate. He laughed. They stayed that way as a new noise entered the morning and a tank rolled along the river road, followed by a line of trucks, their beds crowded with young men. They were passing through the town. Noi and Alisak stepped aside, covering their ears, uncertain about what was going to happen as the great tank lumbered by, almost crushing the crate Alisak had dropped. Then one of the men fired his rifle into the air, and a few others followed.

They waited. But that was all. The men looked down at Noi and Alisak and then at Prany, who had woken and slipped on the hat, and the men passed, all the engine noises unbearable and then growing fainter as the birds circled overhead and the line moved away, heading south. The shudder of the road and that old tree where the basket weaver would notice them four days later, convinced they were spirits up on a branch.

Now, when Noi returned to the ward, the woman had slipped back into her morphine. Even so, Noi sat with her for a little while, knowing that she would always wonder why the woman had called for her earlier that night, would always wonder what she had found in those brief corners of lucidity in her collapsed mind. And why that desire to share it with Noi.

She reached for the woman's hand and held it. She said, "I wanted to tell you that I remember the potter and his wheelbarrow. Once, when I was tired, when I couldn't feel my legs anymore because we had been walking for hours, my brother over there took the wheelbarrow from him, told me to get in, and pushed me down the road we had been wandering. Ten seconds of this act of love and mischief from my brother. Twenty, maybe. The potter, who had been heading to his home from the town before we had come upon him, chasing us. I can still hear the clatter of clay pots around me as I held as many as I could to keep them from breaking. And my brother's laughter even in his own exhaustion. The high canopy and the uneven road . . . in the next life, I hope we will all see each other again."

Noi then said good-bye and navigated the rows to Alisak,

who was still asleep in the corner, not far from the gap in the ceiling. She watched his stomach rise and fall, the twitch of his foot from a dream. The temporary peace of him lying there. She let him sleep a little longer and found Prany taking off the stained bedsheets from a day-old attempt at surgery. Her brother continuing to work in these last moments.

She said, "Soon," and he said, "I know," and she headed back down the hall of mirrors, stopped, faced her reflection. She was unable to remember the last time she had looked at herself in a mirror. Sixteen years old. Her shoulders and her hips a little wider than four years before. There was all the tiredness contained around her eyes. The cracks in her lips. Her hair long enough to braid and tuck under her shirt whenever she drove the motorbike. Her bandanna and men's boots.

She knelt to retie the boots and crossed the kitchen, where a doctor and a nurse were beginning to empty the cupboards, and went up the main set of stairs into the room with the painting and the empty bed frame. She lifted the floorboard and took out their backpacks and slipped the pistol under her waistband. She checked each bag and made sure they were stocked with all their supplies and zipped up. She strapped one on her back, the other to her front, and carried the other out into the piano room, where she was about to kick open the bottom panel of the instrument but hesitated. She thought of baskets swaying from a pole.

The sky shuddered. Out the window, it was growing pale, not quite dawn, but light enough that she could make out the silhouettes of the helicopters approaching. Almost at once, the sound of them was everywhere, and she hurried down. The nurses were already helping the wounded who could walk past the dining room into the blown-out wing where they kept their bikes. She could now hear nothing but the helicopter blades. It came in every gap and hole in the house and was so consistent, like an endless current of the fastest water.

She ran to the bikes, met the force of the wind, dropped a bag beside each, and came back to help bring patients out. Someone touched her shoulder and she turned to see Prany behind her, a woman leaning against him, her eyes alive and unable to settle. The woman was shouting, but they couldn't hear. All together, they hurried to the second helicopter and did one more round.

When they came back to their bikes, Alisak was there with Vang, who told them where they were going. Noi gave the nurse who was riding with her the backpack and then she slid the pistol around her waistband so that it was resting against her belly button. She leaned over to her brother, placed her lips against his ear, and told him to be careful. The salt taste of her brother's ear that reminded her, unexpectedly, of the back of their father's neck. Prany rolled his eyes. All their hair wild and tangled in the rush of wind.

How much they loved these bikes. How much they were looking forward to France. And yet how little, she thought, they knew of it. Noi sensed the nurse settling behind her and said, "I'm going to buy a chandelier," but the nurse couldn't hear. She tapped the nurse's arms to indicate that she should hold her tight. And then they all started their engines, heading out, Prany in the lead and Alisak in front of her, leaving this house forever.

The helicopters were now gone, and the noises of the world returned. The bikes' engines. Her own breathing. She shouted back to see if the nurse was all right, and the nurse replied. Then almost immediately it began to rain. It came down on them, wetting the grip on her handlebars. She sensed her front wheel slipping slightly from the mud but kept the bike straight and pushed on, knowing the rain wouldn't last. She concentrated on the safe line, on Alisak and Vang not far up ahead in the cone of her headlight.

Soon, the sky cleared. She could see the start of morning. Another farm in the valley and then a pair of distant bombers on the bright horizon.

What was that song Vang had been singing?

There was the delay of passing thunder. The engines of their motorbikes. She thought of her brother pushing her in that wheelbarrow as fast as he could. And a silver tray, undiscovered in that house somewhere, with her fingerprints on the bottom of it. Then the map Vang always wanted them to envision as he took them on a verbal tour of French monuments.

She wondered whether the journey would feel far. Or if it would be as though no time had passed at all. Whether there would come a point where this, here, and everything that had happened before would seem so distant she would not be able to remember all of it. And whom would she be with then? Would there ever come a day when she would wake to find that all the pieces of her life and her environment were there as she had left them the night before?

Do you still have parents?

She had woken one morning on that hill to the voice of the peddler who was looking for her and her brother.

She was thinking of the clatter of the peddler's wares, the burned wood smell of him as he leaned down and told them he had found their father when, in the wind and that cone of her bike's headlight, in the growing daylight across the valley, she caught Vang sliding away from Alisak's bike. Her breath escaped her, and she swerved, hard, gripping the handlebars, leaving the safe line of sticks, her bike speeding across fresh earth.

She had turned too fast, was going too fast, her focus still on Alisak and Vang, when she felt the wheels go over a bump. She was searching for Alisak. Her eyes were, frantically. That anchor. And then she found him, looking back at her, and she focused on him, his face, which carried an expression she wasn't certain of, but which seemed to her, in that moment, like the greatest gift, like something wonderful and old, as though, like some unrecognized promise, they had been given a chance, all of them together, to become old. And as Noi let go of the handlebars and the nurse leaned into her, screaming, it was, just then, in all that sudden, immense quiet, enough.

KHIT

(1994)

Tape #1

[*the sound of a piano key . . .*

There is a centaur. In the city, near the station.

Is that how you think of him?

No. I just wanted . . . it reminded me . . . the window, the house . . .
I'm sorry.

You're tired. You've come all this way.

I slept a little on the train.

You must forgive my English. It's gotten better over the years be-
cause of the hikers, but I feel self-conscious about it.

It's better than mine. I know some French.

We can meet in the middle, then. I'm sorry about the train. It is
like that down here, often late. Probably not like that in New York,
no? I've never been. Crossing the ocean, even a small strait, was some-
thing I always wanted to do. And now you are here, having traveled
more than I ever have and ever will. All because of him.

Yes.

It was a lifetime ago.

You said he was here for a year.

Yes. Only that.

A year is a long time. How long have you been here? Were you here before he came? Are you from here?

I thought this was about Alisak. Why is this machine between us?

Would you like me to turn it off?

No, it's all right. But why?

Because . . . in case I forget.

You mean, in case you never find him. In case this is the end.

Will I find him? Where is he?

Why should I tell you anything? You're a stranger to me. I don't trust you yet. And I certainly don't trust that thing between us. Besides, there's really nothing to say. It was more than two decades ago. I can hardly remember myself from those days. Are you sure you don't want to rest? You've come all this way. Here. Drink. The tea is getting cold. I'll get food. How about a sandwich and some olives?

Try.

I'm not sure what you're looking for. He worked for us and then he left. We never saw him again.

Try . . .   ]

She arrived in the spring, landing in Paris and taking the train south through a country she thought she would see seventeen years earlier.

The whole trip took just over a day. She slept in fits and starts, first on the flight over and then the train. She gave up on sleep and walked the corridors of the cars, wanting even in her jet lag to consume everything racing past the windows. She kept a hand in her pocket the whole way and rubbed the cover of the passport she had, that morning, used for the first time in her life. How, waiting in the border control line, she had grown convinced someone would pull her away. That someone had been looking for her all this time. That it ended here.

It was well into the afternoon when she stepped out of the Perpignan station, facing a rotunda where there was a statue of what she thought at first was a horse rearing up. Then she noticed the head and the torso of a man. To her surprise, a group of monks appeared, the bright color of their robes snaking across the street as they paused to take a photo of the centaur.

When a taxi pulled up, she gave the driver a piece of paper with the name of a mountain hostel and in her rusty French she managed to explain how to get there, though he waved the directions away, said that he knew, called it the "old Vineyard."

"You'll need more than that," the driver said, pointing to her bag, thinking she was a climber.

She could barely understand him because of his accent. She looked back at the monks one more time and tried to think of something else to say, to hear him again as he drove down an avenue lined with palm trees. Sometimes, she spoke French with people who came into the restaurant. But there had not been many times since she had immigrated. She had to race to learn another language—English—as fast as possible.

Now, here in southern France, she felt like a new immigrant again. If she had ever stopped feeling like one.

She didn't say anything else to the driver. She caught him glancing at her through the rearview as she checked the front pocket of her bag for the recorder and the tapes. She kept her gaze out the window. Then, as the taxi sped west out of the city toward Vernet-les-Bains, the mountain already visible, like the one near her childhood home, she thought of a promise she had made almost two decades ago, and of that young girl who had followed a man into an abandoned farmhouse in the hopes of leaving with him.

Khit had left, but not with him. Every day, for seventeen years, like a door that would never shut, she had thought of that.

•

"You said you found us through Karawek," Marta said.

They were sitting across from each other at the dining table of the main house. Khit nodded. She said she discovered Karawek through some people she had met. Which led to Marta and this house and how Karawek used to work with them. She was told it was Karawek who had driven Alisak here the day he arrived.

"Discovered her?" Marta said.

"I was bussing a table at the restaurant," Khit said. "My parents' restaurant. We live in a college town. We spent five years in the city, in Queens, and then moved north. It was cheaper, quieter. They opened a Vietnamese restaurant across the street from the campus, in Poughkeepsie. The Hudson Valley."

Marta asked why it was a Vietnamese restaurant.

"It's easier to draw people in," Khit said. "No one would eat there if we called it a Lao restaurant. During the school year, it's popular. The summers are slow. Harder for us. But we manage. We've done okay. I love it there. The beautiful river. The color of the fall leaves and the apple orchards. The light."

She then told Marta that last winter she was working when she overheard a conversation about someone who used to help people in France. It was a table with parents dropping off their kids. They called the person "The Saint." They were talking because of the news. It was on the news.

"You must have heard about the camp," Khit said.

Marta had. "Thailand broke down a camp and sent a hundred refugees back after all these years. It was because they didn't want to deal with them anymore. What do you think happened to them as soon as they touched Lao soil?"

Khit thought it was possible they were arrested and questioned. She said, "Will you think less of me if I told you that I avoided the television when I heard? I didn't want to know. But these people came in that day and they were talking and that was how I found her, Karawek. They asked about the college town and whether their daughter would be all right. Whether it was possible for her to avoid the city—they were referring to the bombing at the World Trade Center last year, nervous that it could happen again. Then they gave me a number I could try that might lead to another one and another one."

"And eventually you found her," Marta said.

Khit had stood and walked over to the piano. She didn't turn but knew that Marta was still studying her, still considering her and what she was sharing. She hadn't known what to think when she picked up the phone and dialed. It was a Marseille number. She didn't believe Karawek would answer. Or be the person people said she was. But the woman confirmed she used to help the refugees. And that she knew Alisak. Karawek admitted all this casually. It surprised Khit.

"Come back to the table," Marta said. "The piano is out of tune, anyway. Is it true you knew each other as children? That's what you said on the phone."

"No," Khit said. "I knew someone who knew him as a child."

"It's hard to imagine what Alisak was like as a child. Who is this person you knew?"

"A man named Prany. They were in the war together."

"How old are you? Of course you wouldn't have known Alisak. You look like a child yourself."

"I'm thirty."

"And when did you come?"

"Fifteen years ago."

"Straight to New York? To Queens?"

Khit shook her head. She hadn't gone straight to New York. She spent two years at a camp in Thailand like the one in the news, she said. She lived in a hut with a dozen others. She fished. She mended tears in clothes and she and the other children attended classes in a large, open shelter run by a teacher. For two years, that was her life. She thought she was heading to France, because everyone else seemed to be.

There were days, she confessed, when she wasn't unhappy there. They had very little food. They were often sick, but they had hope. A point to look forward to. And they had crossed the border. They were safe. They were waiting for sponsorship and they were safe.

"Auntie took care of me," Khit said. "I'm sorry. You wouldn't know who that was. She did what your Karawek did, help resettle refugees, among other things. She visited as much as she could. It was Auntie who convinced a young couple to pretend I was their child because it would be easier for families. And she was right. A Methodist church in Queens sponsored us and brought us over. We got a studio apartment in a large brick building in Jackson Heights. We slept together in the corner, trying to get used to the space, the sound of the heating pipes during that first winter."

"This young couple . . ."

"I call them my parents because they are. They raised me. They're healthy, still working. What time is it over there? They should be heading over now and getting the kitchen ready. I should be with them. In Laos, they were at a mountain hospital helping wounded Hmong fighters during the war."

"Like Alisak."

"Yes," Khit said. "I suppose that's right. And Prany, too."

"And you have been looking for him all this time? Alisak?"

"No, not always," Khit said. Sometimes, she asked around. But as the years passed, it seemed impossible. No, more than that: it seemed insane. To find one person in a continent across the world. Not knowing if he was even there anymore. If he was alive. The insanity of a promise, she said.

"A promise you made to this man . . . Prany."

"Yes."

Marta leaned back in her chair. The afternoon light fell on her and then a shadow from the window behind Khit. Khit didn't turn.

"During his first month here, he was scared someone would come for him," Marta said. "Alisak was. He would wake, convinced the person was close by. He said he had done something terribly wrong. That he had messed up. That he hadn't followed the route, that he had left people in a field. It was like a fever. We didn't know if any of this was true. And now you are here and today I suddenly believe him more than I believe in anything. Is Prany the one he was scared of?"

"I don't think so," Khit said. "No. I don't know."

"Should I be scared of you?"

"No."

"And tell me, you're here because . . ."

"Because I promised."

"The insanity of a promise."

"Because I need to know."

"Know what exactly? That a man named Alisak lived here? That he got better or didn't? That he remained a broken thing or got healthy again? That he made a life with whatever was left in him? Even now, I cannot fathom the amount of bombs that were dropped there. How many did you come close to stepping on? Or witness go off?"

Marta touched her own face, indicating Khit's scar, but she ignored the gesture, leaning forward and wrapping her hands around the warm teacup. The steam glanced against her chin.

Where they lived, Khit said, near the college, there was a middle school with a baseball field. Her father took her to a game one evening not long after they moved. It was free. They had never gone to a game in the city. They sat in the back of the bleachers and shared a paper cone of shaved ice. She loved that their tongues turned blue. It was the first time she saw a baseball up close. Someone hit a foul, and it landed near them.

"That sound," Khit said. "Something happened inside of

me. I couldn't control it. I clenched my fists and began to breathe hard and I shut my eyes. I felt my father holding me, but I couldn't stop. I am sure people noticed. I wanted to stop. I wanted to open my eyes. My father tried to get me to go, but I also wanted to stay. So we stayed. Eventually it passed. But throughout the game I was afraid of the baseball. Afraid of watching it being tossed in the air and afraid for the person who had to pick it up. But most of all afraid of the sound it makes when a bat hits it or when someone catches it in their leather glove. This seems silly, yes? But I was afraid. My father was, too, I could tell. That is the size of a bombie. One baseball."

•

She took a bite of the sandwich Marta had made for her, trying not to stare at the woman, knowing the woman was staring back. She thought Marta was no older than fifty. Even though it was spring, she was wearing a shawl and a heavy sweater, and her hair was braided. There was a moat around her. Khit had sensed it when she had arrived earlier, the way Marta was preoccupied with unwrapping a new paintbrush as Khit followed her inside. The tea already on the table.

Every minute it seemed impossible that they would keep talking, but they did. Perhaps it was her tiredness, but Khit found herself not minding the questions Marta kept asking, and not minding her own answers to them. Other than her family and the customers, she couldn't remember the last time she had really spoken to someone. Her parents were older now, so that most days it was her at the restaurant, closing up. There was the occasional ice cream at the place across the street if it was still open. The college student working there to pay his tuition always giving her an extra scoop. The short walk home to the condominium a few blocks away that she had moved back into years ago and where her mother would be up, waiting for her, watching television. The rare night when they stayed up, remembering Auntie together.

"How long were you married for?" Marta said. "If you don't mind."

"Two years. Long enough to have a child. Javi, he's my ex-husband."

"What does he do?"

"He's a policeman. But farther north now. Near the Canadian border."

"My father was a policeman!"

"Were you always afraid he wouldn't come home?" Khit said.

Marta said she had very few memories of seeing him when she was a child. Something happened in her village and in the surrounding area, which caused him to be gone a lot. So most days, she would listen closely to the radio, hoping to find him in there. She would slowly switch channels wondering if someone else had spotted him.

"He was a bit famous," Marta said. "In the village. Because of what happened. He was by then, how you say, a detective."

Khit asked what had happened.

"He did his job. He solved a crime. But I was asking you about your policeman, not mine. Javi."

"Yes," Khit said. "You're right."

One day, she was on her motorbike heading toward the train station. Every month, a deliveryman would drop off supplies or packaged noodles they got cheaply, so she would go down to the platform to receive them. The man stepped out of the train, handed her the box, and went back in. As she turned, Javi told her to drop it. He appeared out of nowhere. He thought it was drugs. He made her open the box, and to his surprise it was plastic utensils. She began to laugh on the platform. She called him an idiot. He should have arrested her for that, but he didn't; he followed her to the restaurant as though she were going to do something else with the utensils.

"You drive a motorbike?" Marta said.

Khit smiled. "Of course. We all do. My family. It was all we had at the camp. It was our only way of moving from one camp to another, of heading down into Chiang Mai. Six motorbikes. We all learned. We were thirteen, fourteen. The adults taught us. We had to concentrate on how to maneuver the machine on mountain roads, in the mud, over stones. The driving made us forget where we were. It helped us when we were feeling scared or helpless."

There was a man, she recalled, who used to cry every morning when he woke in the camp. As though every day he remembered where he was, and he would cry. Everyone could hear. It was unbearable to so many of them. Not knowing where they were supposed to be. Would they eventually go back home? Were they waiting to go somewhere else? Was this all there was? This mountain camp in Thailand? On a bike they didn't often think about those things.

"But that was how I met him," she said. "A box, a train platform, and a bike. Javi started coming to the restaurant for lunch. He stayed for exactly half an hour always. He would sit by the window alone, order his food, and read a book or do a crossword. I had never seen someone underline words in a book before. Every time he did that it was like he was drawing on me. I felt it. It was strange. It made me curious. I got sick of him eating alone. So I began to sit with him, not caring that my parents and the other customers were watching."

"What was he underlining?" Marta said.

"Passages in novels. It was a way to keep up with his English, he claimed, though really his English is better than mine."

He liked books, she told Marta. He wrote poems he refused to ever share with her. It turned out they briefly lived only a block from each other in Queens. He had emigrated from Mexico as a young boy before her. Then his father found a job at the college as a landscaper and a gardener, so they moved north.

Marta asked what Javi's father was like.

Khit said she never met him. "He died," she said. "Of cancer. A few years before we met. But after those lunches, Javi and I began to spend more time together. He would pick me up after his shift and we would watch a movie or take a walk around the college campus that looked like an amusement park to us, everything so perfect. The hedges, the paths. We stole flowers, telling ourselves it was in honor of his father. We ran into a million students and some invited us to their parties, probably because we looked young. And you know what? Sometimes we went. What do they call them? Keggers. I love that word. It sounds reckless. Javi, the policeman, at a kegger. We did silly things like that. Boys would come up and ask me about my face and I'd make up stories: a knife fight, a boxing match, three pit bulls. Whatever it was, they believed me.

"You see, I was less hesitant then. Less shy of this new world. Less, I suppose, afraid. We made each other laugh, Javi and I. We got to know each other through laughter. He helped me with my English. We were suddenly in a college town in America and we found it both hilarious and amazing. He was alone. Save for my parents, I was alone. We had each other and then we had Philip."

"Philip," Marta said.

"Our child. We named him Philip. We thought it would be easier for him that way. To have a name like that."

"Has it been?"

"What?"

"Easier for him?"

Khit paused. She noticed the tape was running. She made to turn it off, since she had been using it up talking about herself, but then changed her mind. Marta noticed, but didn't say anything.

"I don't know why it didn't work out between us," Khit said. "Between Javi and me. Or I can feel it on some days. It is strong and certain. It is like the feeling when you are aware of the last hour of the day and you haven't done enough, but it is okay. It is okay. I loved him. We had good years. We had our boy. We had an apartment near the train station and the river with bright sunlight and we slept to the whistles of those trains and woke to the smell of the Italian bakery down below. We had jobs and we had my parents, who grew to trust him. We had days off and day trips and a camera and too many photos of Philip. It was a life. A good life. Then Javi left, and I let him. I let him go, because I could only go so far with him. And I don't know why that is. Whether it will be like that with someone else. Whether it will always be like that. I don't know what there is to say that could explain this better."

"Maybe you did already," Marta said.

•

An early star appeared above the far trees. Then two figures emerged from the distant barn and washed their hair using the hose. Khit watched through the window as the water arced up into the dark blue air. The way they helped wash each other.

It was hard to describe, but she was both tired and awake. She wondered if that was what jet leg was. Being in a state of two things. Two places. Here, but still somewhere else.

She wondered if Philip was helping make the takeout kits. When he wasn't at school he was always there and he liked doing it, wrapping the plastic utensils in a napkin and then binding them with a rubber band. He liked peering over the counter and spying on the diners, too. Making up stories about them, which he would whisper across to her. She didn't realize until now how much she would miss waking him from the chair he always fell asleep in and walking with him back home tonight. She lifted her plate to bring into the kitchen, wanting to stay in the thought of Philip for a little while longer, but Marta gestured for her to stay.

So Khit switched tapes as Marta mentioned that it had been a hostel for years. It was for people climbing Canigou and those passing through on their way up the Pyrenees. It wasn't busy right now, but it would be soon. She didn't charge much. Enough for petrol, to keep up the house, to keep the cupboards in the barn stocked with provisions, coffee. There was Yves's garden. She could still manage that. She went once a week into the town.

"Every year I think I will stop, but I don't," Marta said. "I like looking out the window, too. I sit where you sit, wondering about their lives, all these people who want to climb and hike the length of a country."

"It's just you?"

"Just me," Marta said. "Yves died, years ago. He lived long enough to be perpetually annoyed by the hippie campers, as he called them. He missed the clinic. It was more his nature. Our perpetual doctor. The man who once wanted, when he was told he was sick, to operate on himself, convinced he

would be able to cure himself. Stubborn, cocky fool, that Seabird. Did you know his brother?"

"I didn't know he had a brother."

Marta lowered her eyes and then tapped the table. She said
that it was his house they were working in and stuck in. The
children. Alisak. Prany. They were stuck because the Americans had bombed the main roads to cut off the advance of the
Pathet Lao and the North Vietnamese through the Plain of
Jars. The only ways in and out were through small routes in
the valley that they had to make for themselves.

"With the motorbikes," Khit said.

"He was happy there," Marta said. "Alisak. He admitted
that to me one day. He said it like it was a great secret. I think
a great part of him was ashamed to think that. It was wartime.
How old is your boy?"

"Eight."

"They were sixteen, seventeen. They were still just children. Children hired to help others survive a war . . . It's hard
for me to imagine . . . Forgive me. I was talking about Yves's
brother. He fled in the middle of the war, but he left everything behind at the house. All his furniture and art. They were
estranged, the brothers, so we never knew where he went. I
think out of everyone he was the most broken of them all. I

think he harmed others, but Yves was never sure. Or didn't want to know."

"Harmed?"

"I think the broken break. He was in the Second World War. Like my parents. And he survived it like them, and then he spent years living how he did across the world in that valley. Yves was too young for that war. So he was at home, here, in Canigou. He would go for long walks and get lost so that one of his parents or a farmer had to go find him."

"My son," Khit said. "He had a dream last week that he found a cave up in a mountain and he asked me in the morning what happened if you left a dream you wanted to stay in. I didn't know the answer to that, but I told him to keep thinking of it and maybe he would find the cave again on a future night. I just realized that I don't know if in his dream he went back to the cave. And I never asked if in the dream he was ever afraid. I think I am always afraid and don't know that I am."

"You said 'afraid' earlier."

"That it will end. That it will all go away. That I am back in an abandoned house starving and exhausted, pleading with a stranger to take me with him. Or I am back in those years before, unable to walk anywhere, my legs trembling, terrified of where to step, not knowing if I'll trigger a bomb that could take out my feet or shoot up into my groin and up my torso and come out of my mouth as though I had spit it out . . . afraid to walk anywhere, but sometimes having to do more than walk because someone has seen you and wants to talk to you, looks at you that way and promises he has food or clothes or whatever they say . . . Tell me where Alisak is."

The telephone began to ring in the other room. They stayed where they were across from each other at the table, not moving until the ringing stopped.

"If it's important, they'll leave a message," Marta said.

"I left you a message."

"You did. And I called you back."

Khit nodded. "In New York City once, I overheard a man talking to himself at a pay phone. This was in Jackson Heights. I was probably sixteen."

"A block from Javi," Marta said.

"That's right." She said the man was speaking Lao. Other than her parents, Khit hadn't heard it in months. They didn't see a lot of Lao or Hmong in the neighborhood. She rushed up to him, this man at the pay phone, and asked if he knew anyone in France, and if he did, whether he could send along a message. She said Alisak's name. She didn't remember his face but she remembered his shoelaces were untied. She gave the man her apartment telephone number and her address, in case he heard. The man asked if she had any spare change for the phone and Khit gave him the coins in her pocket.

"Later," Khit said, "coming home from school, I found the same man in front of my apartment door, banging loudly. No one was home; my parents were working. A neighbor was peering out, quietly watching. A Korean woman who worked at the wash and fold. I remember a red dish towel always draped over her shoulder. She spotted me and motioned me to hurry into her apartment. Which I did. Then the two of us peered out and watched as this man kept banging on the door, yelling that he was given this address because it was his new home, his now, to please let him in, because the girl who had been living here was dead."

Khit grew silent. Now she heard footsteps upstairs. Marta did, too. Together, they listened as the sound became louder and came down into the open space, Khit utterly convinced there was someone else in the house.

But it wasn't anyone at all; it was Marta's dog.

"How did you get back in?" Marta said. She opened the door to let the dog out again and they watched as it trotted into the distance, moving from field to field.

"Is Alisak alive?" Khit said, looking outside.

"Oh, I have no doubt."

•

Seeing the dog made her miss the strays in Phonsavan. There were days when Khit remembered them more clearly than anyone she ever knew or any one person she tried to get money from or stole from or was hiding from. How those animals would hook their heads over her knee as she sat, all of them tired and dehydrated but keeping her company. Their patience as she attempted to untangle their matted fur or wipe their paws, knowing it wouldn't matter as soon as they bounded off to their alleys and corners.

What did dogs remember? She spent four years on the streets with them convinced they remembered her from when her father, who had given up hiding, with almost nothing left in him, brought her to the border of what was left of the woods and told her to hide behind a tree as a Pathet Lao truck approached. The dogs there sentineled around the trunk as though already sensing the future before she could.

"You didn't leave the town after," Prany had said, when they were together in the farmhouse. She had told him about her father. Whatever fire had been in Prany when they met had suddenly vanished in that moment. She sensed a vacancy in him. It terrified her at first, as though she were blind in the dark, as though it would also happen to her one day, but she had reached for him instead. She would always remember that. Five seconds where she held his limp hand beside a piano, the two of them on their knees, looking down at a floor covered with objects he had taken from the dead.

"Be good," her father had said that day as the military truck approached and he moved away from the tree and the strays. "I won't be long."

Where would she have gone?

She and her father had been on their own for so long that Khit knew no other world. Prany she knew for only two nights. In two nights, Prany helped her do what she couldn't do herself after her father vanished. And all these years later, walking up to a house in southern France, past a rotting bench and a tree, Khit remained unsure why Prany had helped at all, unsure whether she would ever find an answer. She kept seeing him slip a doctor's coat on her shoulders and brush dirt off the lapel. Then the shadow of him behind a window as she turned once to look back at him and never did again.

When the door opened and she followed Marta inside, she spotted the piano in the far corner, identical to the one in the farmhouse in the Plain of Jars, and breathless, Khit almost ran to it.

•

There was a knock. The man who had been washing his hair was standing in front of the house. He asked if there was more coffee for the barn kitchen. Turning to Khit, Marta said that she would be right back and accompanied the man down to the barn, carrying a box of provisions.

For the first time since she had arrived, Khit was alone. The solitude in the new place made her shy. She remained by the table, then moved again to the piano. Then, when Marta didn't return, she wandered the house, shaking off the stillness in her body as she explored and tried to imagine a life here: Marta's, Yves's, Alisak's. The books and the small television in an office down a short, wallpapered hall. Two cans of paint stacked on top of each other in a corner. A flower vase was drying, upside down, by the sink, and there was a large colorful painting of hills hanging on the kitchen wall.

At the camp, her new future, her parents' futures, all of them, had been determined by a single sponsorship. They had been waiting to go anywhere. Now she wondered how different the days would have been in a place like this. She wouldn't have learned English. She would have never met Javi. There would be no Philip.

There were four rooms upstairs. She tried to guess which one had been Alisak's, but was unable to. They seemed anonymous to her. Whether that was because of the years or intentional, she couldn't say. All the beds were made. Each room had a dresser and a closet and an empty vase on the nightstand. She guessed the room with clothes on a chair was Marta's and avoided it, then went in. There were some old photos, photos of Marta's parents, she thought. She sat on the edge of the bed. The room smelled of herbs.

"Alisak is on the right. I am on the left."

Marta was leaning against the bedroom door. Khit apologized, getting up, but Marta ignored her and gave her a photograph. The photo was of three people leaning against a seawall. The tall one in the middle with his arms over the other two. Marta said it was taken in 1970, the summer.

In the photo, Marta, young, was standing with one foot up behind her as she scratched an itch on her calf. Her hair wild in the wind and her eyes nearly invisible. Even then she had a moat around her. But the camera focused on the tall one. It was impossible not to. He swallowed them and the sea behind them. It was the way he stood there, knowing that he did. He was someone who didn't know how to be alone. And Alisak was on the right, leaning into the man, shy of whoever was taking the photograph, of perhaps all of them, but not uncomfortable as something out of the frame caught his attention. More handsome than she had imagined, and in that moment when the camera clicked, sure of himself.

As she kept looking at the photograph, Khit sensed the environment between the two of them shifting. Marta seemed to relax. Perhaps it was because it was her own room. As though Marta were shedding something—that moat. She spoke more softly now:

"He called us his motley crew. His ragged bunch. He said that a lot. Yves. It used to make Alisak smile. His motley crew, his ragged bunch. He was the country doctor, Yves. We were essentially his nurse practitioners. About five of us. It was a clinic for the farmers in the area. Mostly it was for treating broken bones and stitching up cuts. Though on occasion a gunshot victim would come in, his arm filled with pellets. It was often a family quarrel of some kind, though they would claim it was a hunting accident. Two brothers trying to kill each other over an animal, property, maybe a girl. Yves kept the clinic going for as long as he could. He almost went broke. It was his family home, as I mentioned. Where he grew up. Him and his brother. Shall we head back down?"

She took the photo back from Khit and they returned downstairs. The tape recorder was still there on the center of the table. Khit turned it back on.

"You never told me what happened to him," Khit said. "The brother."

Marta didn't know. Yves didn't either. The brother disappeared. But Yves knew some of the staff at the farm who had worked for him, Marta said. Some of them ended up staying when the war reached that area, fighting or working for a doctor over there whose name she couldn't remember. Alisak only mentioned him once. But that was how Yves got word of what was happening at his brother's house. Of what was happening to the country.

"That would have been before they were at the house," Khit said. "The kids."

"The truth was that he was trying to get the people he knew out," Marta said. It had taken too long. Years. They all died or, like Yves's brother, disappeared. Then Yves heard there were teenagers there working as nurses, so he decided to sponsor them and try to bring them over. That was how we met Karawek. She had been living here already in Marseille.

"What was she doing in Marseille?" Khit said.

"She's a painter! Landscapes. There is one in the kitchen."

Then Marta told her that for a long time, Alisak didn't leave the property. He needed the borders of it. Like a coat to wear. But that it was Karawek who first convinced him to come out with them on the weekends. So she would arrive with her fingernails stained with oils and drive all of them to the coast. She always brought her camera along.

"Alisak was uncertain of all that water that wasn't a river," Marta said. "Where there wasn't a far bank. He would wade in and hurry back to the beach, not wanting to go farther in. I was the opposite. I wanted to swim out for as long as I could. I would keep going, and when I couldn't feel my limbs, I would stop and see him in the distance, waiting for me on the beach, as though afraid I would just keep going.

"You know, Yves had a soft spot for him. Because, I think, of his own estranged brother. As though Alisak had carried here some of his brother's house in him. Supposedly, there were three of them trapped in that eccentric house in the Plain of Jars. The girl died. They lost track of the other one. That must be Prany. So tell me. What happened to him? And who was the girl?"

"The girl was Prany's sister," Khit said. "They called her Noi."

It had been Auntie who had told her about Noi. It was on the night Auntie helped Khit cross into Thailand. As they walked through the Plain of Jars, the woman kept talking to pass the time. Khit realized only years later that Auntie had been expecting Prany to be there beside her. But it was Khit. He had paid instead for Khit.

I'll come visit, Auntie said, and for the second time in her life someone older than her said words she wanted to believe but knew were not true. They crossed the valley and then she was placed in the back of the van and was driven away toward the border to Thailand. She remembered the weight of the doctor's coat she was wearing that someone would steal from her in forty-eight hours. And Auntie waving. The small figure of this woman by the side of the road.

"But you see," Khit said. "She did come visit. Every week, she came to the camp. She kept her promise. On occasion bringing somebody else, a terrified orphan child clinging to her as she entered the camp. How she always spent the night. How she always checked in on me. How we talked."

"Who was the first?" Marta said. "The first who said something to you that you wanted to believe, but knew was not true?"

"My father. My first father."

"And what did he say?"

"He said that he wouldn't be long."

•

Later, Marta asked if Khit had ever gone to the hospital during the war. She poured them wine and brought out olives. She lit a cigarette and slid the pack across, tapping her ash on a teacup tray.

Khit said she hadn't, but her mother had been taken there.

They had been separated. She was with her father, her biological father, looking for her. Both of them unaware that her mother, exhausted and wandering the valley, had stepped on an unexploded cluster bomb.

"One of them drove out, picked her up, and returned to the hospital," Khit said. "Fast enough so that she didn't bleed out. Her legs, you see. Her stomach. The shrapnel. They saved her life. Or kept her alive for as long as they could there. Prany told me all this. We were cut off, my father and I. We never saw her again."

"Noi," Marta said. "That is a nickname. A common nickname in Laos. It means small, yes?"

"That's right."

"I remember a few things from Alisak. But he never spoke of those two. Or rarely. Another ocean he didn't want to step into. Or didn't want me to step into. But, he said once that Noi was braver than both of them."

"You say brave," Khit said, "and I think of those kids, those teenagers, driving across minefields all for a little bit of money when, or if, they came back. I think of my biological mother, whom I have no memory of anymore, lying on a cot, and I hope the three of them, Alisak, Prany, and Noi, kept her company."

Khit looked down at the recorder and then at her hands. They heard a distant airplane and they let it pass.

"Does it ever bother you?" Marta said. "That you live in, and are now a citizen of, the country that bombed your first?"

She said she didn't think about it as much anymore. She didn't want to. They got out. They lived.

She said, "I think of my son. What kind of life he will have. Whether he will ride a bicycle or play baseball. Whether he will have a family of his own one day. Whether he will be happy and healthy and safe, and whether he will carry in him the sadness I carry. I think always of my mother, my biological mother, and whether she died alone. I think of Prany and wish he were here. I think of all the stray dogs I left behind and I think of the ghosts."

"The ghosts?"

"Do you believe in them?"

Marta lit another cigarette. The smoke swirled up toward the ceiling light. She didn't answer, but told Khit that on Alisak's first night here, he ran away. Or walked away. She had insomnia. She was outside on the bench. He appeared from the house, went past her, and stopped by the tree. He was facing the clinic, and she thought he was about to walk down the slope. He didn't see her yet. In the moonlight, he looked so much younger than he was. She had just turned twenty-three. Yves had a birthday party for her the week before and there was a cake stain on her shirt. She had been rubbing it, looking at him, trying to gauge him. Alisak was a stranger to her and yet in that moment he was also like a phantom, spectral, floating across and down.

But he didn't go down. He turned and walked straight toward her. He was humming something she couldn't remember now.

"But I remember," Marta said, "that he took my face in his hands very gently, and I didn't know what to do. I looked back at him. It was like he wanted me to. And then he walked across a field and began to climb the mountain. I should have, but I didn't follow him just then. He had frightened me. I couldn't tell if he wanted to kill me or ask for my help. I looked into his eyes and it was like there was nothing anchoring him. I didn't want to see that. I didn't look as he climbed. Eventually I went in, tried to sleep, and when I opened my eyes it was light. First light. My favorite hour. When everything feels forgivable. And then I remembered. And I ran. I ran up the mountain trail and, two hours later, I found him at a park ranger station, beside a shed, asleep, curled into himself and nearly frozen.

"He never did that again. But sometimes, we would lose sight of him for an hour or so, though we never knew where he went. It was like there were paths around the property only he knew about. We got used to it. He did his work. He always did his work. He set broken bones and gave shots and listened to everything we said. The farmers lying there would look at him, wondering where he had come from, trying to hide their surprise when he spoke back to them in French. He could suture faster than I could. We used to race using grape-fruits, threading the needle across the skin. Yves would pick one up from the fruit bowl, about to eat it, and we could hear his shouts as thread dangled from it like it was some creature or a kite. He hated when we did that."

The photo was still on the table beside the recorder. Khit picked it up again, studying the three of them on the seawall, Alisak looking slightly away.

It was then Marta said that Yves had an old Honda motor-bike. Alisak didn't know about it until Yves opened the shed one day and asked if he wanted to fix it up. He had to order the parts from Karawek, who picked them up for him in Mar-seille. But Alisak did it. He fixed the bike right up and, she admitted, it surprised her. She knew so little of what he knew, what he was good at, what his history was other than he had come to them needing help, that he could work at a hospital, and that sometimes he cooked for them. It was like he was slowly revealing himself. Or gathering back things he had for-gotten. Now there was this bike.

"He used to stay up at nights with me," Marta said. "Mostly, he listened as I talked. He liked hearing how I hopped trains and hitchhiked all the way down from the north. Which was true. Eighteen years old. Thinking I would eventually hit southern Spain and go farther."

Khit wanted to know why she left home. When Marta didn't respond, she said, "Did you know Alisak would leave?"

Marta replied that except that first night, there were no hints. She woke up one morning and he was gone. Late summer. They tried looking for him. Karawek, too. For a month, they tried. But it was up to him, wasn't it? They weren't forcing him to stay. They thought he took the bike until she saw it back in the shed. He had polished it, had left it for them. Full tank.

"Did you ever drive it?" Khit said.

"Yes. Not Yves. But sometimes I took it out, yes."

"Where did you think Alisak went?"

She thought he might have hitchhiked to the coast. Then maybe headed toward Marseille. Or caught a ride with migrant workers into Spain.

"I asked you earlier if you wanted to know if Alisak got better," Marta said. "I don't think that's quite what I wanted to say. If you are looking for a reason why he left when he did, I can't give you one. If you want to know if he was happy here, I don't know that either. Alisak did his work, as I said. He made us happy. He made me happy."

"You were in love with him."

"I think so. Yes. Once, a very long time ago. In the months before he left, we used to drive out together on the bike, the two of us. The last time we did this, we parked on the coast and climbed over the seawall. It was calm. Really bright. The water was silver. We were the only ones. Here is what I remember: He asked if I could teach him how to swim. I always forgot he didn't really know how. So we took off our clothes and went into the water. It was impossibly calm but we stayed where it was shallow. I held him as he floated on his back and then he flipped over and again I held him. He kept his chin above the surface and tried a few strokes. I remember his arms and his legs moving, and I remember the water and the empty, quiet night, and his breathing. And then we didn't speak. And that is my last memory of him."

•

It was dark now. Marta turned on the lights as Khit changed tapes again. Rather than coming back to the table right away, Marta stayed by the light switch, considering Khit again from across the room.

"Did Alisak ever play?" Khit said. She was referring to the piano.

Marta said he never did. But that it was nice. When Khit

played those notes earlier. Hearing them in this room. It was like a voice she had forgotten about. She wasn't expecting Khit to do that when she first came in. Yves had played.

"I confess I didn't know what to expect when Karawek called," Marta said.

Karawek had long ago stopped doing what she did, but she lived in the same apartment in Marseille from those years. Marta could shut her eyes and still see the geography of it. The tiles and the balcony. The room with stacks of paintings and a dent in the wall from when a man had entered in the middle of the night, shoved Karawek against that wall, and began screaming at her that she didn't take him where he needed to go. That he was utterly alone.

"He hit her so hard," Marta said, "her head broke plaster."

"What happened then?"

"She always carried a knife. So do I." Marta reached down into her boot and placed a knife beside Khit's tape recorder. Then for the first time Marta laughed and returned to the table. "This is my mother's. From her war. My father's war. And Yves's brother's war. If I was short with you when you came, I apologize. I had not thought about Alisak in a long time. Does that disappoint you?"

Khit didn't answer. Out the window, against the night, flashlights appeared, moving high along the mountain slope.

She thought of the dog. And what Philip would think of a house by a mountain.

"You said it's just you now," Khit said. "Did you ever think of going back? To where you grew up?"

"This is all I know anymore," Marta said.

"You never told me why your father, the policeman, is famous," Khit said.

"It's not something he wanted to be famous for."

"What happened?"

"When I was a child, a young woman was found hanging from a tree with a black hood over her face. This was farther down in the valley. Her shoes were found neatly placed together underneath on the grass, the ankles touching, straight toes. My parents knew the girl. She was from a family who bred horses. She was fourteen. It was terrible. I have little memory of this; I was too young, and my parents didn't talk to me about it until I was older, but it was terrible. It changed everything. The valley spent years forgetting a war and then this happened. And then it got worse. A month later, another girl was found hanging from a tree, hood over her face, wrists bound behind her. Shoes set underneath. Now it became a nightmare."

"Your father was on the case," Khit said.

Marta nodded. The mountain communities there were

small. Smaller than villages. They gave her father jurisdiction of all of them, and he worked the case. He was the senior. He was Maquis, in the Resistance, during the war. He was actually from the Spanish side of the Basque country, but he was Maquis. All the villages, she said, they respected him for that. So they made him a detective. He got a partner, and together they worked the case for a year. It took a year.

"I told you," Khit said. "A year is a long time."

"My mother didn't see him throughout the investigation," Marta said. "If he came home, it wasn't him she was seeing. She had never known him during the war, but she thought it must have been that person she was seeing. He hardly spoke. She said once he seemed dangerous. Not to anyone in particular, not to her, but that there seemed to be an element of danger to him suddenly, as if he would explode if she touched him. It almost ruined them. She used to also say she wouldn't know what she would have done without me to care for. But I don't believe a word of that. I think my mother was drunk that whole year, and he knew and didn't care."

"Did it happen again?" Khit said.

"Within that year, it happened two more times," Marta said. "Always the black hood and the wrists bound behind her. The shoes. I'm sure the papers called the man—it was a man—something clever, but I don't remember anymore. I'm sure the valley didn't call him anything clever. It was their life. Girls, daughters, were seen less, so little at times some people thought they had been caught by this man only to realize their parents were keeping them locked up in their farms. It was a nightmare."

"But he was caught," Khit said. "The killer."

"Eventually, yes."

It was because of a cigarette brand, Marta told her. The man smoked an older brand, before the war, that was hard to purchase in the area. He left a bit of it near the last hanging girl. So it started there.

"And your father became famous in the area for it. For catching him."

"Here is what broke my father's heart," Marta said. "It was a fellow Maquis. He didn't know him, but it turned out it was someone who had been in the Resistance during the Second World War. Same as my father. Running up and down this border here between France and Spain, fighting the Germans. A man my father's age. He was reliving a memory. Or mimicking it. During the war, as he passed through a village somewhere, he had seen a girl hanging from a tree with a wooden sign hanging around her neck with *Judin* written on it. The difference was that the ones he killed were from various places and backgrounds, no connection. All he cared about was that it was a girl."

Marta wrapped her shawl tightly over her shoulders. She said her father stopped working not long after. He took up gardening and renovated their house. He bought a bicycle and joined her mother on trips into the village.

"You're tired," Marta said, and leaned forward, almost touching the recorder. "So am I. I'm not used to keeping still like this. Or talking for so long. I've done nothing this evening but talk. Let's take you over. You get to stay here before the chaos of Midsummer."

They stood together, and Khit collected her bag. For a moment, they stayed by the door, as though they were both not yet sure they wanted to leave the room. Then Marta pointed out the window and mentioned that for Midsummer they lit a fire on the mountain above them. And then other fires were lit across the peaks in the Pyrenees all the way to where she was from. So every year, she called her father, waking him, and told him to look out the window at the fire, she was waving. And she didn't know if he was listening or caught in some dream. She never asked what he dreamed about. She remembered great happiness as a child. But there was also a tremendous sadness over there. It never left. She knew it was still there. She knew when she heard her father's voice that it was still there.

"And here?" Khit said.

"You might think this is silly," Marta said, stepping outside. "But I never arrange my shoes anymore. When I take them off, I toss them on the ground and leave them how they are. Pointing in different directions. Far apart from each other."

She was set up on the bottom bunk in the corner of the barn. There were others on the far side. There was a door to a kitchen and along one wall was a long communal dining table where a bright lightbulb was hanging, casting shadows.

A bird had gotten in. Or perhaps it lived here. It moved from rafter to rafter, as though getting used to her. She could hear the sound of its flight. And then voices from across the barn. A woman brought coffee to the table. She was holding a headlamp to look at a map spread out in front of her.

This was the first time Khit had left New York since she immigrated. She was thinking of that. And how the day she met the parents who would end up taking care of her, Khit had gone to the creek near the camp. She remembered the casualness of the meeting, of them walking down and the woman asking if Khit would like her hair washed. How far away she seemed then from the camp. So Khit had entered the water, bent down, and felt the woman touching her head for the first time.

The bird swooped low over the table, and as the woman ducked, the corner of the map lifted slightly.

Restless, Khit stepped outside. In front of the barn, she lit one of Marta's cigarettes. The smoke enveloped her and went pale and floated up. In the moonlight, she could make out the house on the small hill with one window light on. She could make out the outline of the bench and the tree.

There were days when her parents and her son were the only things that made her want to live a life. There were also days when she was convinced it would all go away, that she would come home one day to find that they weren't there, that they had never been there. And then there were times, not many anymore, but still there, some faint echo, when she didn't want to go home at all. That it felt possible to stay away, and away from them, to keep going from one route to another for the rest of her life. And she didn't know why she felt that.

Something brushed her legs. She looked down to find Marta's dog beside her, leaning against her and wagging its tail. She then felt the weight of the tape recorder in her back pocket. It had her last cassette. She pulled the recorder out, brought it to her lips, and turned it back on. She spoke her son's name into the microphone and then said, "I don't think you'll ever listen to this, but I hope one day you do," and rewound the tape.

And so, listening to the last tape, Khit walked around the barn, the dog following, past the coiled hose toward the shed. She opened its door as quietly as she could and turned on the light. She approached the tarp, lifted it up, and examined the motorbike. A moth flew in. She leaned against the seat a little as the dog sniffed the wheels and studied the moth.

When she came back outside, more flashlights were gliding across the mountain. Holding the recorder, still hearing her own voice, and Marta's voice, Khit sat down on the grass, crossed her legs, the dog with her, and watched the night in the fields.

•

Tape #4

[*A cough. A chair shifts.*

Is that really your son's?

Yes. I had to buy it for him for a school project. The assignment was to carry it around with him on a walk and record noises. And then he would try to identify what he had recorded. I went with him. Or, rather, he went with me. We walked around Poughkeepsie and to a park in the Hudson Valley.

Did he identity everything?

I don't remember. I forgot to listen to the recording. He did that on his own. It was so expensive. The machine. I was angry at myself that I had bought it. That the school had asked me to. It is difficult sometimes, as I said, depending on the season.

Do you miss him?

Philip? Yes. Of course. He doesn't know I took it. I took it from his room. The recorder and the blank tapes in his drawer.

How much does he know?

He knows I am here. I told him I had to meet someone from when I was a child. I think he was more interested in the idea of me as a child.

Do you think that is enough?

Enough?

What you told him. To share a life. To call it that. A shared life. Is it honest?

You never married or had children . . . I'm sorry. I didn't mean to say that.

The truth? I feel most like myself when I'm alone. I'm not sure whom I get that from, if I get it from anyone at all.

You never told me very much about your mother.

She was a nurse in Calais. During the war. Then she settled down on a farm in a village called Sem, where she eventually lived with my father. She was a morphine addict, from the hospital she used to work in. She had good years and bad years. I loved her. I think because most of all she survived. She kept surviving. Even survived that year of such sadness in that area. It never stopped her from riding a bicycle every day to the village to have a few drinks at the inn and listen to their old record player. Papa hated that she did that. Because

of what was happening around us. All those killings. She would say,
What would a crazy person want with me? and pedal off. She liked
jazz and she gardened. She had friends, many friends. Spanish friends,
American friends, French friends. I'm convinced they were all spies.
They all seemed to know each other from those years after the war
and I think they formed a kind of family, sharing information. When
she was younger they liked to visit her. I remember the house always
with a guest from somewhere. Always the music and the food and
their talking. I remember their names, I loved their names: Oliver,
Camille, Mikel. The men with their mustaches. The one with a bad
limp. Camille, who always smelled wonderful. Like grass after rain. In
the mornings, a sleepy spy would stumble out of a room, yawning and
rubbing their eyes, surprised to see me, the child, awake and staring
up at them. Mama, she died peacefully, in her sleep.

You miss her.

I miss them all. I miss them all because we never understand how
quickly they go, yes? I miss Papa, whom I never see anymore and who
has very few years left. I miss everyone who used to work here. I miss
Yves, who was like a father to me, a second father. And you here today,
tonight, I miss Alisak the most. He was the hesitant one. We had a
problem with water, once. The city was working on a pipe. I watched
him take out all the bowls in the house and line them up in the closest
field because it was about to shower. It did shower, hard, but what I
remember is how he held the bowls close to him as though they were

flowers. Bright flowers. All that rain and color in the field . . . You never told me what happened to Prany.

Prany . . . yes. He was caught. Three months after he bought me safe passage into Thailand. He was in a van, on his way to give a messenger on the Mekong supplies to bring across the river. A pastor, I recall. A Christian. I don't remember the man's name, but I remember him bringing up food, mostly. Medicine, gasoline. And me always knowing it was from Prany. Sometimes, Prany would hide a small gift for me in one of the boxes. Something from the house, from one of those pouches. How I loved that. How I always waited. Until the day the pastor didn't show up when he was supposed to. Eventually, the van was found ransacked and abandoned on the side of the road. Prany and the doctor—his name was Vang—were charged with the murder of the interrogator and they were executed. They knew Auntie would be at the camp. They sent her Prany's head tied up in a blanket. They had caught the pastor, you see, but they had let him go. They let him go so that he could carry the head back across himself. They probably followed him up to the Thai border but there was nothing they could do after he was across. Maybe they didn't even care about Auntie anymore after this. I think they just wanted to see this man with a severed head on his back, crossing a river, climbing up the mountain . . .

I was there when he showed up. Auntie didn't push me away or tell me to shut my eyes, and for that I am always grateful to her. We dug a small grave behind the hut I was staying in. We only had one trowel, so we took turns and then we used our hands. We stayed very close together, kneeling and knowing what was inside as she untied the blanket one knot at a time. She looked down, but I didn't, I was looking at her. I was looking at her crying. I had never seen her cry. It was the only time. She was so still, but her eyes trembled. Shook. It was like the world had entered her eyes and she didn't know how to contain it. To hold it. We had a bucket of water and some soap, and as she cried, she washed her hands. She made me wash my hands. And then she cleaned Prany as best as she could, wiping the dirt around his eyes, washing his hair. And then we wrapped him in a new cloth and buried him. We never knew what happened to Vang's body . . .

I remember trying to say something to Auntie that day. To have the courage to say something, anything. That I was sorry. That I knew it was Prany who was supposed to come across and not me. That I wanted her forgiveness. That it should have been him here, beside her. But I said nothing that day. Nothing at all. Auntie told me to go dump the water, and I did. And when I came back she was gone, back down to help someone else, and I went to the class I was supposed to be in and learned some more math, ignoring the chemical smell on my hands . . . I'm curious, have you ever used powdered soap? . . .]

•

In the morning, Khit returned up the hill. Marta was already outside, wearing an apron and a bandanna over her head. She

235

had brought out a can of paint and was repainting the old bench. She wiped her brow with the back of her wrist as Khit approached.

A wind came and the tree above them swayed loudly. Below them, down the slope, a group of hikers was at the head of the trail that would lead them around the town of Vernet-les-Bains and up the mountain.

"Sa Tuna," Marta said.

"What?"

"Where Alisak might be."

Marta reached inside the apron pocket and gave Khit a faded envelope. On it was written the address of a coastal town in Catalonia, only ninety minutes south. Then she told Khit it was the last known address she had for him. A room in a guesthouse in the Costa Brava. The Wild Coast, she called it. She didn't know if he had always been there or if he ended up there after other places. She didn't know if he was still there. But years after he had left, he sent her that photograph Marta had shown her yesterday. She thought Alisak must have heard Yves had died. It was his way of acknowledging it.

In Spain!

After all that time, he was only ninety minutes away. She pinned the envelope to the kitchen wall and looked at it every day. Every day, she imagined what his days were like there, living in a guesthouse. What he was doing for work. Whether he went swimming. Whether he had any friends or had met someone. And whether he had found the life he had gone searching for. Every day, she woke up thinking today would be the day she would step out and go visit him.

But the truth, she said, was that she wasn't sure he wanted her to come. And then, as the days went on, she grew convinced he didn't. There was so much to do, to decide what to do, here. She was alone. She didn't want that to be an excuse, she said, but Yves had always been here. Now there was just her. One week folded into another. Then the months. He slipped away. Alisak. The thought of him did.

"Let's go together," Khit said.

Marta leaned down, dipped the brush into the open can, and kept painting the bench. "Do you think it is still there? The farmhouse in the Plain of Jars."

"Yes," Khit said. "I think it is. I think someone else lives there and it is something else."

She watched as the new green coat began to spread along the back.

"One house," Marta said. "One place. All that it holds over time. All the changes. Do you think this one will be here long after we're gone? After I'm gone?"

She didn't wait for Khit to answer. She stood up again,

237

facing Khit, and told her that she could use the bike if she wanted. That the keys were inside the shed.

"I'll expect you back, of course," Marta said.

"I'll come back."

"We'll have dinner together tonight. I'll cook. We'll sit down without your damn tape recorder and we'll eat and we'll talk some more. What do you think of that? And then you'll go home to your family and you'll tell your boy that you stole that thing from him."

"I will."

"We'll be friends."

"Yes."

"You'll visit again. With Philip. With Karawek. You'll come back."

"I'll come back."

"Good," Marta said, and returned to the bench.

The hikers had begun to climb. They were on a slope above the house. Khit went down to get the bike. The wind came again, stronger, and the dog barked. Before entering the shed, she turned to look at Marta one more time: she was kneeling on the ridge, now in the distance, barely visible under the swaying tree.

Khit left that same morning, driving south and crossing the border into Spain.

Not long after, as she made her way down the coast, she came upon ancient hill towns overlooking the water. In one, on a high bluff, there was a medieval castle. A dark wall that crawled over the cliffs. Someone was in a tower. Then she realized it was a stone head of some kind of animal, perhaps from a myth, perhaps a horse, forever confronting the water and the horizon.

She thought of her centaur. What the roads were like four centuries ago. Old animals carrying supplies and wares across the hills. Stucco houses that had now become, some of them, hotels with balconies facing the bays.

Khit was arriving one month before the start of the tourist season. It was colder here, and the hill town Marta had directed her to was empty. She twice drove through its maze of unmarked, sloping roads until she found a way to access the guesthouse. It stood near a bay and a rocky beach.

She didn't think the guesthouse was open—the sign was off, but the door was unlocked, so she walked in to find a narrow lobby and a chipped desk at the far end. Somewhere there was a television on with the news, and in the air was the smell of ashtrays and bread baking.

The man who came out had half his shirt unbuttoned and was picking his teeth with a toothpick. He greeted her in English. She passed him the address Marta had given her. Chewing on his toothpick, he glanced at it and told her that Alisak didn't live here anymore.

Before Khit could say anything back, could ask this man a question, the man pointed out the window behind her, up the slope, and said, "He lives there."

And then he asked if she was a relative, and Khit shook her head, not yet certain if she imagined what he had just told her.

"Are you having problems with your bike?" the man said, picking his teeth again.

Khit didn't understand until she was standing at the other address near the top of the hill. She had passed it on the drive down. It was a shop where tourists could rent bicycles and mopeds to go sightseeing around the Costa Brava. The shop wouldn't open for another hour. She peered through a front window, but the lights were off, and there was no one inside. She spotted only a monthly calendar on the wall with hand-writing under each date.

One hour. It was forever. She headed back down. This

time, Khit skirted the guesthouse and her parked motorbike, and she didn't stop until she was on the rocky beach, close to the water. Behind her, an old man wearing sneakers was taking a stroll on the boardwalk with a newspaper curled up under his arm. Pretending not to be curious about her, he paused to study the menus of the restaurants not yet open for lunch. Otherwise, Khit was alone.

She waited for the sun to come back again. She stared down at her own shoes as if for the first time, realizing the soles had worn away, probably a year ago. Slipping them off, Khit placed them side by side on the rocks, then changed her mind and dropped one haphazardly to make sure they were far apart from each other.

Then, without turning to see if anyone was watching, she stripped down to her underwear and waded into the bay. Her breath was taken out of her from the cold shock of water, but she kept wading farther in, following a line of yellow buoys until the water rose up to her chin and she could no longer feel the bottom. Shutting her eyes, Khit inhaled, dove under. She surfaced and pushed forward. She swam for as long as her body could stand it, and then swam back.

Someone was standing by her pile of clothes. She thought it must be the old man, but as she hurried out, she saw it was a child, a girl around ten or eleven. The girl was holding a towel over her arm like a waiter and was carrying a cup of espresso. "You're a crazy lady," the girl said, in English, and handed over the towel first, which Khit wrapped around her body, and then gave her the coffee.

The guesthouse manager was on the boardwalk, the toothpick still in his mouth, shaking his head and watching Khit shiver uncontrollably as she followed the girl up the beach, her feet unused to the hard stones that were like knives on her soles. As they passed him, the girl said something in Catalan, then called him "Papa," and brought Khit inside to the bathroom of one of the restaurants that were not yet open. It was then that she introduced herself as Isabel and handed Khit her clothes under the stall, one piece at a time.

When they came back, a table facing the bay had been set up for them: more coffee and a plate full of fruit and pastries. The girl named Isabel sat on one end, Khit on the other, and while the father helped a waiter set the other tables, she began to eat, luxuriating in the food and the hot drink, her body warming but her skin cold and coated in the salt of the bay. Out the window, a boat appeared and vanished behind a headland.

"You're here to visit Alisak?" Isabel said.

Taking a bite of a pastry, she told Khit he used to work at a nearby canning factory. That her uncle worked there, too, and that was how they met, her uncle driving him into town one evening, Alisak asking for a room, speaking to them in French.

"Uncle died," Isabel said. "He had . . . how you say . . . a scar . . . on his neck. Like yours. You like fish?" She pinched her nose and said the two of them always stank of it. Then she rested her head on her hand and looked out the window to where the old man with the newspaper was high above them on a cliff.

She went on: "It connects all the towns. The path, up and down. Alisak. He likes taking walks, too. In the afternoons. He always turns. When I call to him as he is walking up. I shout his name, and he always turns and slows. Right there."

The silhouette of the old man looked like a bird about to take off. Then he was gone, around the bend. Khit waited for her to say more, but she didn't; she pulled out a deck of cards and taught Khit a game. They played. They focused on the game until Khit brought out the tape recorder and asked Isabel to say hello to her son. Which Isabel did many times, singing a pop song in English and saying a few words in Catalan and Spanish, phrases Khit didn't understand, but ones that made the girl laugh, head back and mouth open, bits of the pastry stuck in between a gap in her front teeth.

When it was time, Khit began to walk back up the hill.

The guesthouse manager shouted from the street below, "Tell him to come down for lunch," and waved with his chewed-up toothpick. It wasn't until she was almost to the shop that she realized she had been walking barefoot. She caught the faint winding trail of her own damp footsteps, and she paused to scan the coast, the hint of that castle to the north, suddenly understanding that it wasn't the water that was wild, but the coast itself—this unpredictable line of jagged rocks and bluffs as though its other half had broken off and floated away centuries ago.

The Wild Coast.

The shop was open. Connected to the office was a garage with its door lifted up, the space filled with bicycles and mopeds standing in rows. In the back, there was a service station where a man in his forties was on his knees, filling bicycle tires with air. He had yet to notice her, and she didn't go in just yet. She stood outside near the entrance, lifted a hand for shade, and watched him. His quietness and the few lines of gray in his hair. The glasses he was wearing that were connected to a lanyard around his neck and the handkerchief in his back pocket.

Taped to the wall above him was an old postcard of a young woman by a river.

In Khit's own pocket was a small seventeen-year-old piece

of paper that no one knew about anymore. It had been taken from a doctor's coat before that coat had been taken from her, and it had a circle drawn on one side. The paper was so crumpled and worn that it was barely there, but she had saved it this whole time and brought it with her, tucking it into her passport. She was clutching it now like a charm, like it was the only thing she had ever owned, as she listened to the garage radio and the faint hiss of the air pump. The drips of water from her hair as they hit the concrete.

All around her was the daylight and the smell of the ancient ocean. She felt the salt on her skin, the pebbles stuck to the soles of her feet, and tried to imagine the distance from here to all the places she had left behind. Then to wherever she was going. Which one was farther. In this moment, she had no sense of the future. What the days ahead might hold, what happened next. What this man would do when she began to speak. And what, she hoped, they would learn about each other. It was as though a hand had appeared inside her chest, gripping her heart.

She thought of her son. Always her son.

And then a shadow flitted past. The radio went to static. And Khit, taking a step, reached up to ring the bell Alisak had hung on a wooden hook by the door.

SA TUNA, SPAIN

(2018)

He sees today, to his own surprise, like sudden weather, that old hill of his childhood. The deep map of it. A certain path where they—himself, Prany, and Noi—slid down during one rainy season, frightening the animals. All those walls they knocked on in whatever code (what were those codes?) they made up. Or the painted tent where a man used to sell shoelaces and matchbooks, and the hilltop where they built their first-ever successful fire one late night, beyond pleased with themselves.

He turns. From the shop, Alisak has heard a sound. A moment later, a ball appears within the frame of the open garage entrance, bouncing across until it hits the loose gutter of a neighbor's house and stops. He takes off his glasses, expecting someone to come chasing after it. But no one does. There is no other sound, only the morning.

It is as though the world is holding its breath.

So Alisak, sixty-six years old, stands and leaves the garage, passing the rows of bicycles and mopeds, and heads across the street. He looks up in the direction of where the ball came, already self-conscious about the necktie he has been wearing since he had come down to the shop. Then he looks in the other direction.

The street is empty. The distant water flat and calm, only a slow wind. He is standing in front of the homes of neighbors he has now known for decades, each of their doors a different color—blue, orange, yellow—all matching the color of the window shutters. He is aware that it takes ten steps to approach the blue door from his own. That he has never seen Josefa, who lives alone, without her apron that is so frayed it is hardly an apron at all. And that Josefa is the age Alisak's own mother would have been.

The rain gutter creaks as he picks up the ball, which is cold and a little larger than his fist, a child's soccer ball. He tosses it up once as the dark arc of a cat hops down a window-sill farther up the ridge.

"*Gato*," he calls to it. "I suppose this isn't yours?"

The cat vanishes into an alley, and Alisak brings the ball back inside, where he places it on the table beside a gift-wrapped box and his notebook. The pages of the notebook are mostly filled with how the shop has done every season. The names of the customers who visit this town yearly and some detail about them: what kind of bike they liked, an anniversary they were celebrating, a birthmark on a wrist.

He tears off a piece of paper from the back and writes,

in Spanish, a quick reminder to himself to ask around later if anyone is looking for a soccer ball. Isabel, whose birthday is today, will tease him for this when she arrives at her father's place for a party. Tease him because Alisak still prefers the pencil and paper to his phone. News on an old-fashioned radio. He tells her it is the texture of paper, that it feels more permanent to him, but what he really wants to say, and has never said to her, is that for the first seventeen years of his life there were so few times he was given a chance to write anything. He hardly knew what writing was.

His phone beeps. He ignores it. Whenever it makes a noise—whenever, in fact, he writes—he is reminded of Vang, who in another life would have taught Isabel how to play the piano. Would have somehow found a piano for her somewhere in this town, commandeered it, and made sure she practiced. *Loose wrists, no tension.*

Isabel, who is thirty-five this year, has been living in Barcelona and working behind the desk at a fashionable hotel near Las Ramblas. He has never been to visit her, and he doesn't know if she ever resents this. *Oncle*, she has affectionately called him since she was a teenager, using her first language.

He has, over the years, become her ally. And although she has never said as much, he knows he is one of the last remaining links to her real uncle, whom she adored and whom Alisak used to work with at the cannery. The split-second kindness of a man who slowed his car as Alisak was walking down the road after his shift. Two days in, and Alisak had yet to speak to anyone other than the floor manager. And then this man who had worked beside him anonymously, both of them wearing goggles and masks, and pushing racks of sardine tins to the oven, had rolled down his window in that growing dark and asked if Alisak had a place to stay yet. Never once asking where he had been or where he was from.

He thinks now that it must have been Prany who taught him and Noi how to build a fire. Prany was often the one who ventured across the hill as though it were a palace he wanted to know. Coming back with some new knowledge of how to wash their clothes better or a new stray that had joined the pack or showing off a toy he had bartered for with shoelaces. Two spinning tops. A light wooden airplane the size of a fore-arm that seemed to fly forever. They had lost it on the same day as it glided down the river. He remembers that.

It is time to go. Alisak picks up the gift, closes up the shop, and walks. He goes the long way, as he often does, taking the trail that follows the slope down behind the hillside houses, passing arrows on posts that point to other towns, and the occasional red-and-white square of paint on the wall to indi-cate the trail. The morning grows clearer. The wind catches his necktie, and he stops to adjust it beside the stone ledge he likes to sit on to watch the movies the town has begun to show every Midsummer on the bay. The darkening ocean always visible around the story on the portable screen that is large enough so that Alisak can watch from a distance. The music of a romance reaching him. Isabel and her father blinking a flashlight up at him to try to get him to come down.

Forever he will marvel that he has now known this family for longer than anyone in his life. That it was the two of them who were across the dimly lit lobby as he entered the guesthouse for the first time, unsure of the days ahead, the days that had already gone. A father handing him a key and a child no taller than the height of the reception desk, asking if he played cards.

Which is what the woman named Khit mentioned as she stepped into the shop that day so many years ago. How she had just played cards with a child before finding him. And how it was funny that he had left one hill to settle down in another. And then she told him why she was there, her words and the names of people he had once known quickly unspooling like the thread connected to a kite, as Alisak tried to grasp all that she was saying, and then did.

He wonders, wherever Khit is now, whether she thinks of him anymore, the way he sometimes thinks of her, thinks of the time they spent together and their conversation. The way he will sit by the table among the bicycles and listen to what is around him as though she never left. As though she is forever leaving for him a small piece of paper that she thought belonged to Prany—she wasn't sure, but she had kept it, had made sure to keep it, in case it did belong to him.

And he wonders whether there will come a time when he forgets that he placed that piece of paper in his nightstand drawer, in a pencil case he has never once opened after that day. And whether the forgetting will ever bother him.

He thinks he might, just once, stand this year, clink his glass, and say some words at the birthday party.

Cars are now pulling into the guesthouse below. Alisak recognizes the last one and knows he should hurry down the trail; he had wanted to be there before she arrived.

But he doesn't hurry. He holds Isabel's gift with both hands, and as he looks across at the far, bright southern towns along the water, there is that hilltop again—the sound of animals and the river moving below, and the matchbook they keep throwing into the night. Three children fighting sleep so that they can catch the last moments of a small pocket of fire.

Acknowledgments

All facts and figures in the author's note were taken from Joshua Kurlantzick's *A Great Place to Have a War* (Simon & Schuster, 2017); the websites of the BBC and the Mines Advisory Group; and a 2016 speech made by President Barack Obama in Vientiane in which he acknowledged America's role in the war and committed further support in safely removing, and disposing of, the UXOs that still remain buried throughout the country.

I have significantly altered the geography of Laos and the time line of the war—in particular, the bombings on the Plain of Jars—to suit the purposes of the story. Although the town of Phonsavan exists, the one here is entirely a fiction. As is the area around the Canigou in southern France where I placed "the Vineyard."

The paragraph on pages 101–102 on "natural resources"

257

ACKNOWLEDGMENTS

and "self-sufficiency" is a combination of an October 24, 1976, *New York Times* article, "Laos after the Takeover," by David A. Andelman, and a paragraph from Grant Evans's *The Politics of Ritual and Remembrance: Laos Since 1975* (University of Hawai'i Press, 1998). The descriptions of the billboards at the bus station are based on photographs in the same Evans book. The dialogue about "Party and Government" on page 102 is a recollection from a camp survivor, Thongthip Rathanavilai, from Evans's *A Short History of Laos: The Land in Between* (Allen & Unwin, 2002). The paragraph about "optimism" on page 76 is from the same book. The mention of Laos being a "domino" on page 155 is a quote from President Dwight D. Eisenhower. I am also indebted to Vatthana Pholsena's *Post-war Laos: The Politics of Culture, History, and Identity* (Cornell University Press, 2006) and the poems of Mai Der Vang.

The centaur Khit refers to is Nessus. The statue is not in Perpignan but in the Tuileries Garden in Paris. The image of the movie playing on the bay on page 253 was inspired by a section in an essay by Ralph Sneeden, "Blaenavon," published in *The Common*.

•

I want to thank the National Endowment for the Arts for their support during the writing of this book. My deepest thanks also to Alexander Maksik, Colombe Schneck, Stefan Schaefer, and everyone at the Can Cab residency in Spain, where I wrote parts of this book. I would like to thank as well Arthur and Sarah Evans, Chris and Deirdre Caldarone, and all the Crooked Laners in that corner of Massachusetts where I was given time and a room of my own.

Thank you especially and always to Ralph and Gwen Sneeden, who are family to me.

Thank you again to Christopher Lin. And again to Christopher Beha and everyone at *Harper's Magazine,* where a portion of this book was first published.

For their kindness, enthusiasm, and dedication, I am again indebted to everyone at Simon & Schuster, most especially Zachary Knoll, Kayley Hoffman, Carly Loman, Amanda Lang, Elizabeth Breeden, and Jonathan Karp.

Marion Duvert, Simon Toop, David Kambhu, Lilly Sandberg, and Griffin Irvine at the Clegg Agency: exquisite minds, grace, and fire.

Marysue: everlasting gratitude for your faith, guidance, friendship, and brilliant light.

Bill: my beloved friend, mentor, brother, fierce wonder.

Laura: to this great, vast journey with you.